STORMY WEATHER & OTHER STORIES

MERCER
UNIVERSITY PRESS

Endowed by
TOM WATSON BROWN
and
THE WATSON-BROWN FOUNDATION, INC.

STORMY WEATHER

& OTHER STORIES

Lisa Alther

MERCER UNIVERSITY PRESS

MACON, GEORGIA

MUP/ H851

© 2012 Lisa Alther
Published by Mercer University Press
1400 Coleman Avenue
Macon, Georgia 31207

First Edition

Books published by Mercer University Press are printed on acid-free paper that meets the requirements of the American National Standard for Information Sciences—Permanence of Paper for Printed Library Materials.

Mercer University Press is a member of Green Press Initiative (greenpressinitiative.org), a nonprofit organization working to help publishers and printers increase their use of recycled paper and decrease their use of fiber derived from endangered forests. This book is printed on recycled paper.

Library of Congress Cataloging-in-Publication Data

Alther, Lisa.
Stormy weather and other stories / Lisa
Alther. -- 1st ed.
p. cm.
ISBN 978-0-88146-386-6 (hardback : acid-free paper)
-- ISBN 978-0-88146-366-8 (e-book)
I. Title.
PS3551.L78S76 2012
813'.54--dc23
2012021535

Stories in this volume have been previously published as follows:

"Squeamish," *Claymore* 1 / 2 (October 1977): 7–14.
"Termites," *Homewords*, ed. Douglas Paschall and Alice Swanson
    (Knoxville: University of Tennessee Press, 1986).
"The Fox Hunt," *Appalachian Heritage* 32 / 1 (Winter 2004): 13–22.
"The Eye of the Lord," *Iron Mountain Review* 27 (Spring 2001): 6–7.
"Encounter," *McCall's* (August 1976): 103-11.
"Wedding Belles," *Sunday Express Magazine* (London: 1999): 33–34.
"Stormy Weather," *The Best of the Best*, ed. Elaine Koster and Joseph
    Pittman (New York: Penguin Putnam, 1998): 1–24.
"The Politics of Paradise," *Louder than Words*, ed. William Shore (New
    York: Random House, 1989).
Birdman and the Dancer, with monotypes by Françoise Gilot
    (Copenhagen: Gyldendal, 1993; Amsterdam: Contact, 1994;
    Hamburg: Rowohlt, 1996).

For my daughter Sara,

Vermonter born and bred

CONTENTS

SQUEAMISH

It was sweltering that night as I sat in the stairwell in my pajamas, watching smoke drift from the living room on a ray of lamplight. The calico cat slunk out of the shadows and paused to stare at me, green eyes flashing, then narrowing in recognition. She leapt up the steps. I scratched her ears until she turned her head to lick my hand with a sandpaper tongue.

The newspaper rustling in the living room punctuated the pulse of the locusts outside. My father's large frame would be filling the brown leather armchair, and his fingers would be flicking a cigarette. My mother would be curled up on the couch with a library book.

My father's voice rumbled like flexed tin roofing. Hearing my name, I scooted partway down the steps, purring cat still draped across my lap.

"I don't think he's too young," my father was saying. "I could ride a horse to hell and back when I was his age. But too squeamish—maybe."

"He's just sensitive," said my mother.

I frowned.

"It's not like I'd just toss him in the saddle and turn him loose. I'll teach him first."

"I tried to ride for years but never felt I had any control over a horse," replied my mother.

Back in bed, I remembered walking through the woods one autumn afternoon, crunching every red leaf I came to. I was halfway running because my father, holding my hand, was walking at his own pace. Then he dropped my hand to raise his rifle. Something white and brown plunged out from behind a bush. He turned, following it through the sight. The animal rose to leap over a fallen tree trunk. There was a sound like a stick breaking. The animal jerked, scrambled forward, and then collapsed.

I was running. Branches were lashing my face. I squatted and looked down. Red was soaking the white and turning the twitching tan to dark brown. The orange and yellow leaves were splattered with red. I shivered, clenching my teeth.

My father's mouth was moving, but I couldn't understand what he was saying.

"...it didn't feel anything at all," I finally deciphered.

He paused, waiting for me to reply. But I couldn't.

"If we don't shoot some of the deer, they'll all starve to death in the winter." He pulled me to my feet and put his hands on my shoulders. "You have to learn to be tough, Winston. To make things best in the long run. You can't be squeamish."

Blotting sweat off my forehead with my top sheet, I listened to the bullfrogs croaking down by the pond and to my father's soft snoring from their bedroom. Squeamish. It sounded like what it meant—sick and shivering, like squirting blood.

I remembered standing on a stool one time, wearing a long green gown that hung down around the stool so that I seemed seven feet tall. Everything was a murky undersea green—the walls, the backs of the nurses and doctors in their scrubs. I stood on tiptoe, craning my neck. Finally, I saw it—a meal for a monster. Red, with globs of yellow fat. Silver probes were picking and digging. Pale rubber hands dabbed with bloody gauze.

I couldn't breathe. I tried to pull off my mask.

My father murmured, "Get him out of here, Alex. I never should have brought him in."

The lights lurched back and forth. Alex set me down on the green-and-black-checkered linoleum, saying, "I guess you don't want to be a doctor like your dad and granddad?"

I crumpled to the floor.

That's what squeamish meant. But I hadn't felt like that since. Now that I was older, I understood why you had to cut people open. Because it was best in the long run.

A couple of days later I hopped on one foot down the stone steps out front, imagining I was a war hero with a missing leg. As I rounded the house, I spotted a large brown horse. I stopped and stood very still, hoping it wouldn't notice me.

My father was smiling. Not taking my eyes off the horse, I tried to smile back.

"Where did you get that?" I asked.

"Her name is Vera. She's a retired show horse that one of my patients sold me. Think you can handle her?"

"Sure." I tried to sound nonchalant.

"Ready for lesson number one?"

I nodded warily.

"You have to convince her that you're in charge." Holding Vera's forelock in his fist, he worked the bit past her teeth. "They don't like this thing in their mouths. You have to leave them no choice."

I touched the velvet between Vera's nostrils. She nudged my hand in a silent pact against my father.

He tossed a saddle on to her back. After buckling the girth, he paused a moment, then wrenched the strap a couple of notches tighter. "They puff out their stomachs when you fasten the cinch, so that the saddle slips when you try to mount."

I looked into Vera's dark eyes. I seriously doubted that she would play such a nasty trick.

My father climbed into the saddle. "Break me a switch off the apple tree."

I did, also breaking my pact with Vera.

"Show it to her."

Her ears pricked forward and her nostrils dilated, making me feel like a heel.

My father whacked her with it, and they circled the yard. He put her through her gaits, explaining how her leg movements shifted with each one.

My grandfather used to ride horses into the hills where cars couldn't go, and my father went along to keep him company. He described stopping one afternoon in front of a shack roofed with rusting soft-drink signs and old license plates. The lathered horses waited in the yard, which was cluttered with empty tin cans and bottles. Two bluetick hounds howled and hurled themselves against their chains.

Dodging some clucking hens, my father and grandfather crossed the porch. Inside sat a dozen people of different ages, men and women, all with deep-set eyes and high cheekbones. Nobody said a word. The stench of infection was strong. My father held an old man's trembling arm, while my grandfather drew an injection into a needle. The old man, face furrowed with pain, sank his broken teeth into my father's arm. Like a snapping turtle, he refused to let go. No one moved a muscle. My grandfather finally pushed the old man to the floor. Those teeth marks were now pinpricks on my father's forearm.

My father stopped the horse in front of me. "She's getting old. She's a little sluggish." He dismounted. "But she's beautifully trained. You just have to let her know what you expect from her."

I sat straight and still in the saddle. I'd always liked horses. I used to draw them—purple and orange and green horses that flew through the air and swam underwater. I'd checked out all the horse books in the school library. The horses always loved the kids that owned them, saving them from forest fires and outlaws and other dangers.

Every summer at the carnival I rode my favorite plaster stallion, ivory with tan spots and a gilded saddle. He moved up and down on a chrome pole, while the engine in the middle throbbed and hissed. I held the reins with only one hand, smiling indulgently as younger children all around me clung to their poles in terror.

I'd been on a real pony once at the fair. He was smaller than Vera, but I was taller now, so it came to the same thing. My father could ride when he was my age, so I knew I could, too.

"...and be sure to grip with your knees. Now try walking," said my father.

Vera jogged for a few yards, driving my backbone into my brain.

"Keep the reins taut," said my father. "And pull back smoothly, don't yank. Her mouth is tender."

Vera threw her head forward, and the reins slid through my palms.

"But don't hesitate to be firm!" called my father.

I was now bouncing in the saddle, as though riding a bronco.

"Don't try trotting yet, Winston!"

He apparently didn't realize that wasn't what I had in mind either. As I slid sideways, I grabbed at the pommel. A necklace of pain encircled my throat, and I hit the ground hard.

Above me the wire clothesline twanged slowly back and forth across the blue sky. My father came running.

I stood up, swallowing to be sure I still could. "It's okay," I croaked. "I'm fine, Dad."

"What's wrong with you, son? When she tosses her head like that, pull it back in!"

"But you said her mouth is tender."

"That's why you can control her with the bit. She's got to know who's boss."

"But if she really wants to take off, there's nothing I can do about it," I realized.

"We may know that, but she doesn't. Unless you let her find it out."

You could count on running into something if you rode a horse around your backyard. That's why I had spent a week clearing a path through our land. I sat on Vera outside our rosa multiflora hedge. The noon sun was hot, and the saddle I'd carefully polished gleamed like glass. Vera was damp with sweat. Flies circled us, trying to dodge her tail and settle on her twitching muscles. I tried to shoo them away before they bit her.

We started toward the dam that formed our pond. Vera twisted her head. She wanted a drink. But my father had said never to let her eat or drink once she was saddled, so I kicked her with my heels. She shook her head, making the bridle clank. Then she lunged toward the shore.

Water rushed up at me, soaking my jeans. Vera writhed on her back like a Holy Roller, burying my leg in the mud. Gasping and choking, I dragged myself out from under her.

The mud came off the two of us, but later that afternoon I was still trying to wipe the orange clay off the stupid saddle. I could have yanked her head around and lashed her with my whip. That's what my father would have done. Well, that's what I was going to do from now on. It didn't matter whether she liked me or not. I'd show her who was boss. I scrubbed furiously at the leather.

The next morning at breakfast my father cleared his throat, pushed back his chair, and lit a cigarette. The cat rubbed against his leg. He pushed her toward the door with his foot. She returned, purring. "We've decided to sell Vera," he announced. "And maybe try again later. When you're older."

He was looking at my mother. He could ride when he was my age. He didn't really think I was too young. He thought I was too squeamish. So did she.

"Please don't sell her, Dad. I'm just catching on."

He looked at my mother. She was staring at her plate.

"What makes you think so?" he asked.

"So far I've been nice to her, and she's taken advantage of me. She doesn't realize how tough I can be. But she's going to find out."

My mother looked at me doubtfully. She opened her mouth, then closed it.

My father nodded. "Okay, let's give Vera another chance."

I carried my dishes to the sink. He wouldn't be sorry he was giving me another chance. I went outside and grabbed the bridle. I walked up to Vera and forced the bit between her teeth. I fastened the strap at her throat. I hoisted the saddle onto her back. After yanking the girth tight, I scrambled up, tapped her with my whip, and guided her through the gate.

When we reached the pond, she turned toward the water, which sparkled in the sun. I jerked her head around and whipped her hard. She trotted along the dam.

Riding wasn't really that hard. You just had to show the horse who was boss.

As we skirted the tobacco field, grasshoppers in flight whirred all around us. Entering the woods, we made our way past ribbons of sunlight that threaded through the mesh of poplar branches overhead. Vera's hooves thudded like a heartbeat on the dark dirt. A mockingbird jeered from a nearby pine.

We entered the alfalfa field. Past the farthest hills rippled the Blue Ridge Mountains, scalloping the sky with hazy blue-gray.

I realized we'd been standing still for several minutes. Vera was munching alfalfa. Down at the barn one day I'd heard some cows bleating in agony. My father had said, "They broke into the alfalfa field and gorged themselves. It would be like you eating a quart of ice cream all at once."

I hauled in the reins. Vera threw her head forward, and I pulled it back in hard, saying, "It's for your own good, Vera."

She snorted and shook her head, clanking her bridle. Clenching the muscles in my jaw, I raised my stick and swatted her flank. She stood quite still, as though astonished. Then she plunked one foot in front of the other and skulked across the field.

As Vera and I descended the sloping meadow, the ochre foothills rose up to hide the distant mountains. Soon we were in a valley formed by a rushing creek. A barbed-wire fence separated the alfalfa from the creek, where cows in the opposite pasture watered. They had worn a path alongside the creek down to the milking parlor by the barn.

It was cool and dark there by the stream with the willow branches hanging low. Everything was silent except for water swirling over the moss and through the cress.

Vera and I followed the fence, hiding from the sun, until we came to a fork. We could take the left path and climb a low cliff, or we could stay by the water. I turned Vera up the cliff. She stopped and eyed the hill, and the scorching sun at the top of it. She veered toward the stream. Shrugging, I let her continue down the valley.

The path was rutted by the hooves of the cows in wet weather. But Vera, refreshed, began to trot. I tightened my knees and tried to post. But I wasn't very good at posting yet, and Vera's gait had, in any case, accelerated to a cross between a trot and a canter.

I tugged on the reins. She tossed her head, her mane flowing out behind her and stinging my cheeks. She surged forward into a canter. I felt a thrill in my stomach like when I pumped really high in a swing. I lay alongside her neck and let her run.

From the corner of my eye I could see the parade of passing fence posts. This was crazy. I should stop her. The path was too rutted. She could break her leg.

Up ahead the cliff jutted into the path, forcing it against the barbed wire. A wave of fear swept through me, and I pulled in hard on the reins. Vera just tossed her head and hurtled on. There was no way she could know the path was too narrow for us to get through. I was the only one who knew. I was the boss. I sawed at her mouth with the reins. She shook her head like a spoiled child, dancing playfully on her delicate ballerina legs.

Her whinny was a shriek almost human. Sharp knives sliced my leg. Vera twisted diagonally, wedging herself between the barbed wire and the cliff. She plunged up and down with panicked snorts. Red was splattering everywhere. I felt myself slipping off the saddle. The entire world was upside down. A dull thud as my head hit a fence post turned everything to black.

It was drizzling out the window. The leaves on the branches were just dying and falling off with no final flourish of fall color. I sat by the fire in the living room, my leg propped on the coffee table. I had a lot of stitches and a couple of pints of someone else's blood.

I wanted to go to the barn. But I was only out of bed on the condition that I not walk. I knew my father didn't want me to see Vera. But I could see it anyway: the soggy straw splotched with stinking purple ointment. An olive army blanket with Vera's head sticking out from under it, her eyes closed and her breathing jagged. And underneath, the gashes. The jagged broken bone in her leg that would never heal. I shivered. Squeamishly.

I heard a crack like a dead limb breaking off a tree. A little later my father's boots stamped on the stone steps outside. Looking up, I saw him in the doorway, wiping rain off his rifle barrel with a rag.

"She was very sick and could only have gotten worse," he announced, not looking at me.

My mother, standing behind my chair, put a hand on my shoulder. "It's not your fault, Winston," she said.

My father looked at the two of us for a long time. "No, it's not your fault, son," he finally agreed.

TERMITES

I hate to be the one to mention it, being her only child and sole support and all. But Mama's getting senile. No doubt about it, to my mind.

First signs are last month, just before spring up and decides to break over here at Beulah. I could tell it was coming—spring, I mean—because the termites had started in to swarming. Don't know what it is about that front porch, but you wouldn't believe how those termites flock to it. Why, last spring they gnawed right through one of those front columns. I mean to tell you, sawdust was just a'flying ever which way.

Well, the porch roof was fixing to fall in, so Mama had me out there hammering boards on the pillar till we could think what to do about it. She wanted to replace it, but I thought that was real silly myself. Well, we know whose is the hand that feeds her, so I don't need to tell you that those boards is still up there this spring. Well lord, you can't keep a termite from wood. So this year they start in on the boards.

Anyhow, it was a lovely afternoon, irregardless of tiny winged demons of destruction all over our front porch and lawn. I'd come home early. I work down at the Beulah Basin Hospital for Dr. George Roller, Sr. Been with him near twenty-five year now, I reckon. Ever since I come back home after that summer in Knoxville. I'm selling tickets at the Rebel Theater when Mama catches up with me. I'd rented me one of those tourist cabins out on Bloody 11-W, with a screened-in front porch where you can sit and watch the wrecks. I got free entrance to the theater on my time off, plus all the free popcorn I cared to eat.

Then Mama calls up to say that Daddy is passing away and what do I want to go live in a city for anyhow. So I go on back home, and that's when I start working down at Doc Roller's.

I was going to say that this particular day I'm speaking of turns out to be a real busy one down at the office. I brew Dr. Roller's coffee. Then Ida Faye, the lucky lady who works for that good-looking Dr. Alex Standish, comes in bringing me some of her seafoam divinity. Well, we sit around eating that till we're ready to puke. Then I order me some red plastic gladiolas from this discount catalog to kindly decorate up the office with. Then I type that week's "Beulah Basin Bulletin." That was my idea—a sheet ever week for the patients, announcing births and deaths and accidents and what have you. So's people can know to send flowers and cards and all like that. Dr. Roller has such a degree of good faith in me that he just leaves the entire thing to my doing.

Well, who sashays in then but the little Renfro girl (the one marrying the Sturgiss boy next month) demanding can she see Dr. Roller. I leave the door open a crack so's he can call me if he needs to. I happen to be working in a file cabinet by the door, so I hear him talking to her on the subject of the marriage bed, and her acting like it's all news to her.

If you ask me, that girl should've been educating *him* on the topic. I used to wonder didn't Mrs. Roller have cause to fret over him and me being alone together there in that office year after year. Till I come to see that that's the least of her worries with him. It's not no normal man can look at naked women all day long and not never pay no mind to his own secretary.

Dr. Roller like to knocks me over with the door as he opens it. He says, "Felicity, I don't have anything further for you to do today, so why don't you just go on back home?" So I thank him, pin on my hat, pull on my white gloves, and pick up my patent leather pocketbook.

When I get home, I close my eyes and run past the termites fast as I can with my eyes closed. Inside, Mama has the shades drawn down tight. Keeps it cool, she says. I don't know about that, but I do know that's what kills her houseplants—and not me, like she always claims. Well, it's been so bright out that I don't see a thing, but I'm sure she's setting around somewheres talking to her dead relatives in the dark. So I call her, but she doesn't answer. The house just kindly creaks and echoes some. I figure she must be out to her Daughters of the Confederacy meeting.

I decide wouldn't anything be nicer than to sip a little something up in my room till she gets home. Nothing more pleasant after a hard day than setting up there with a refreshing beverage reading the *National Enquirer.* "My Husband Doesn't Know I'm a Man." Lord, I love a good exposé.

So I go out the kitchen door and around to the storm cellar, where Mama's been saving this here champagne for my whole life long. Used to say all the time how it was for my wedding.

Well, my single state is her entire fault. I had a boy one time that was real sweet on me. We used to sit in the parlor after Mama got Daddy quiet for the night. I'd let him kiss on me, and I'd generally let him feel me some. But Mama found out all his daddy did was run Doc Roller's farm up near Big Lick, and that was the end of that. I said at least his daddy worked, unlike some I could mention. And she said, "Hush, child. Your daddy comes from family." Like the rest of us was hatched under laying hens or something. She looked me up and down and then she said, "Your daddy's a wonderful man, and don't you ever forget it, little lady. He never has a bad word to say about you."

Law, I remember the girl that boy finally married. Ugly little tow-headed thing from somewheres up North. Mrs. Roller had a tea for her when they first come back to Beulah, and she turned out to be real nice. I told her so. I never was one to mince my words. I says, "Honey, you're a real nice little thing. But why do you reckon Ned, Jr., had to go all the way up to New Jersey to find him a wife?"

I didn't bear him no grudge. Next time I seen him on the street, I says, "Lord, Ned, it don't matter one bit that she's not real good-looking because she's such a sweet little thing. She don't even sound too much like a Yankee." And he seemed real appreciative that I'd forgave him like that, and he just grinned at me like a panting dog. I always was one that gave credit where it was due and didn't nurture no spite.

Well, anyhow, they is no use in letting all that good champagne go to rack and ruin there in that damp dirt cellar hole. I have long since made up my mind not to wed. I don't aim to spend my life waiting on some deadbeat drunk like Mama did. So I take a bottle ever now and then when she's not around. Just moldy old bottles anyhow. I toss the empties down the laundry chute. They end up over in some corner of the basement nobody's visited in years.

Poor Daddy. I remember one night shortly before he went to his reward. His room was right smack under mine. He'd just stuck his hand into the chute with his empty when mine crashed into it from up above. He thought the hand of God had dashed it from him. ('Course his stuff was a good deal stronger than mine.) So he goes stumbling across his room just a'hollering for Mama: "Pristine honey, I have received the summons to judgment for my transgressions!" Then there's this crash, and I don't hear anything further from him. The only summons he ever got was all those times for drunk driving.

Like I was saying, this particular afternoon I get over to the cellar door when I hear Mama's voice out back by the cemetery. She like to haunts that place, cleaning up the graves and growing ground covers and all like that. And she sets up displays with her great uncle Travis's medals and sword.

14

Sometimes she hangs up what's left of his grey uniform, so's it looks like a scarecrow. On pretty days she raises his regiment flag. She says he sacrificed his life for the South and deserves this much from his own. Personally, I find it real curious that succumbing to measles at Lookout Mountain constitutes a holy act.

She normally asks me to help—like I don't have enough to do as it is. Besides which, I don't care none about them folks, whom I didn't even so much as know.

This particular afternoon I can't imagine who she's talking to out there. I wonder is she sure enough gone batty this time. So I head on back out there. I see her standing there shaking her pruning shears in the air. She has her red baseball cap pulled real low so's her hair sticks out straight on all sides. And she keeps stamping her plaid tennis shoes like she's crushing termites. She's fit to be tied.

I get near enough so's I can see two little boys almost hid behind Travis's tombstone, which is carved to look like a weeping willow tree. The bigger boy is holding Travis's sword in both hands. Their eyes and their mouths are open about equal. They've just moved in a few blocks away. Their daddy is down from Massachusetts with that hose mill that's going up on all sides of our house. Law, they offered Mama the moon. Said up at Boston they tear down tenements like ours quick as they can, factory or no factory. That's what they called our house—a tenement.

After that Mama just absolutely refused even to speak to them. Carpetbaggers, she calls them. So I reckon they're just gonna let her see how she likes living smack dab in the middle of the worker's recreation area. Just to the left of the baseball diamond, so I hear tell.

Mama's voice is grating like somebody after an operation on their voice box: "...and don't think you all can come in here trampling and pillaging our very graves. We're not beaten down here. We're just resting." She shakes those shears like a tomahawk. The little boy waves the sword at her like a lion tamer's chair. Then Mama plops down on her uncle's marker and starts bawling to beat the band.

The little boy drops the sword and drags his brother through the hole in the hedge. I lead her towards the house. Then, to top it all, she turns and stares me up and down like I'm a freak in some carnival sideshow. And I have to ask myself if those termites haven't started in on her brain. Because when you start pitching fits for no reason at all, that pretty well proves that you're getting hard in the arteries, or soft in the head, one. So that's why I'm being forced to consider putting her in the county home. Though I just hate the idea, you understand.

THE FOX HUNT

The Jeep shuddered along the dirt road, its hood bobbing like a duck decoy on rough waters. Sunlight danced through the rust and mustard foliage.

Palmer felt like a kid laying out of school. Even if he did own the company. But he was, after all, out here on business. Julius was an expensive dog. His ancestors had been lead hounds for the best hunts in Virginia, right back to the beginning of the nineteenth century. But Lucas had implied on the phone this morning that Julius might not make it.

He and Lucas rode away from the clearing, Julius hanging across Lucas's saddle, his neck ripped open and oozing black blood.

"We'll take him to that vet in Beulah," said Palmer, who had raised Julius from a puppy and helped Lucas train him.

Lucas shrugged. "Ain't no use."

Palmer sighed. Lucas always turned as fatalistic as a European peasant in the face of a crisis. "Don't be ridiculous. He'll be fine."

Reaching the top of the rise, Palmer surveyed Red Hatcher's bottomland, spread out below like an old burlap feed sack. That soil there along the riverbank used to be pretty rich, but you couldn't say much for it now. Looked like he'd sown winter rye, just sprouting. Red drove his land as hard as the antique tractor he worked it with.

The Jeep jolted down the hill, the power lift on the back clanking. Palmer spotted some fresh stumps and brush piles in a woods Red was leveling for more pasture. That man razed rather than cleared. He didn't plow, he gouged.

Four boys in bib overalls marched up the valley, tobacco-stake rifles on their shoulders. Palmer was leading, his Confederate great-grandfather's sword hanging from his waist, scabbard tip etching the earth.

"Halt-two-three-four!" barked Palmer. "All you men down in that trench on your bellies!"

The boys peered into the drainage ditch by the rosa multiflora hedgerow as the enemy closed in.

"On the double!"

They jumped in, sinking to their knees in mud. Palmer crawled beneath the hedge to inspect the advancing Yankees.

Red's carrot-colored crew cut appeared above the lip of the ditch. "Ain't you comin' down here too, Palmer?"

"Head down, soldier! Do you want it blown off?"

Red leapt out of the ditch. Twisting Palmer's arm into a hammerlock, he forced him to the edge. "Palmer—sir, I ain't playing at your goddam game no more." He hurled Palmer face first into the slime and stalked off down the valley, swinging at grasshoppers with his tobacco stake.

Gazing at Palmer with vacant blue eyes, Lucas Bledsoe helped him out of the mud. But he didn't reply when Palmer asked, "Why'd he do that for?"

Red's fencing needed help fast. A couple of posts had rotted, dragging the barbed wire to the ground. Last week Red had come up to him by the tobacco barn, struggling to sound amiable, despite the stubborn jut to his red-bristled jaw. "Y'all right today, Palmer?"

"Fine, thanks, Red. You?"

"Tell you the truth, I got me some problems." He slipped a kitchen matchstick between his lips and began to chew it.

"What's up?" asked Palmer, even though he already knew, since he went to Rotary meetings with every banker in town.

"Reckon you could make me a loan? Through the winter? Whatever interest you think's fair." Red gazed at the ancient oaks on the far hillside.

Palmer could see that he was humiliated. But it was his own damn fault. "I'm sorry, Red." He was, too, even though he could see how much better off Red would be in the end. "But I'm no banker. Have you tried the Savings and Loan?"

"Hell, they's a mortgage on ever last one of my damn cows." His bony face began to twitch.

Palmer shifted his own gaze to the oaks on the hill. "My offer still holds: I cover the bills. We split the profits. Cash for your land. Fair market value. Same as my father did with Lucas's father."

"Thanks all the same." Red hurled his matchstick at the ground and strode away.

The fence posts flashed white as Palmer passed from Red's land onto his own. To the right was a field at rest. To the left, Lucas's hired man was disking a newly cleared cornfield. Directly ahead was the barn, freshly whitewashed, and three shiny indigo silos.

Palmer had to confess that he loved his work. He'd turned an abandoned textile mill in town into a shopping mall. Once he'd finished salvaging these forlorn little foothill farms, he'd use part of the land for a golf course, a lake, and a vacation home development for retirees with a taste for country living. At cocktail parties he often quipped that, like Napoleon, his only ambition was to own all the land that adjoined his.

Rounding the bend, Palmer eyed Lucas's maroon-shingled house, which clashed with the orange clay of his yard. He pulled his Jeep alongside Lucas's battered pickup, cut the ignition, and studied the truck that was rusting away like a junkyard soup can.

Palmer walked over to the garage. As his eyes adjusted to the gloom, he spotted snarled rope, rolls of chicken wire, rusted equipment parts, and empty oil cans, all tangled up together.

Palmer and his father stood in front of the newly painted garage. Inside, coils of rope and wire hung on pegs. Paint cans and rotor blades were neatly arranged on shelves.

"Mr. Bledsoe, this is my son, Palmer," said his father.

"Pleased to make your acquaintance, Palmer." Mr. Bledsoe nodded toward a skinny boy in overalls nearly white from washing. "This here's my boy, Lucas."

Palmer and Lucas studied each other. Palmer held out his hand. Lucas just looked at it. Feeling foolish, Palmer dropped it to his side.

Palmer's father said, "Well, I'm sure the boys will have fun playing together when we come out here on weekends."

"Lucas here, he don't generally have him a whole lot of play time. But I reckon we can make him some."

"Mr. Bledsoe, we're pleased to know you, sir. You and your boy."

"Yessir, Mr. Claiborne, and I'm right proud to be working for you'uns."

Last month Palmer had ribbed Lucas, "Looks like you just take a pitchfork and heave anything running around loose into that garage there."

Palmer had smiled, but Lucas just gave him his numb blue stare. "Ain't ourn no more. Don't make no never mind to me what it looks like."

"But you and I are in this together," Palmer had insisted.

Lucas glanced at him sideways, then lowered his gaze to the ground.

Palmer shook his head as though clearing the din from his ears after target practice. Then he walked toward the house, of which the top-floor windows lacked several panes of glass. He'd let Lucas stay on in the house as though he still owned it, so he supposed how Lucas kept it up was his own business.

"Lucas!" he called.

A bald truck tire hanging from a mulberry limb in the front yard swayed silently. He started down the road toward the cinder-block milking parlor. The gravel had long since washed off, and gullies had formed, which Lucas had filled with trash.

The hounds began yapping and hurling themselves against the chicken wire of their pen. Palmer put his palms against the wire and let the hounds lick them, scanning the pack for Julius. Somehow he'd believed Lucas would have come up with a remedy by now.

That morning of the hunt, the riders in their blue and buff coats had gathered in the field beside Palmer's cabin at the foot of the valley. Sitting on their horses, they had sipped wine from plastic cups.

Alvin Ferris called to Palmer, "Where's your better half at, son?"

"Marge refuses to have anything to do with us ever since she broke her leg last September on that jump across Dead Creek. She says we're out of our minds."

"Well, she's correct about that!"

Palmer actually suspected that his wife Marge, who'd put on fifty pounds since college, didn't like to watch how some of their women friends looked at him in his tight, buff jodhpurs, the same ones he'd always worn. She seemed to hold it against him that he hadn't gone to pot along with her. Well, let the old girl sulk in solitude. He couldn't help it that he had some life left in him yet. Raising the antique brass hunting horn he'd bought in England, he played the tattoo that signaled the start of the hunt.

"Let's get on with this circus," he muttered to Mindy Ferris, with the rueful smile she'd found irresistible for a brief period a couple of years ago.

"It *is* a circus." She was struggling to rein in her snorting bay, her thighs gripping the saddle as tightly as they had recently gripped his hips. "That's what makes it so much fun. If we took this stuff seriously, we'd be dreadful."

"You don't take much of anything seriously, do you, Mindy?" he murmured with a mock-doleful expression.

"Nope, I just take life and love as they come. Lucky for you, I might add." She shot him a coy smile.

A couple of riders finished checking girths and adjusting stirrups in the drizzle of the wet fall dawn. As they mounted, the hounds were released from their cages to scurry around the paddock, sniffing milkweed pods, manure piles, and each other's rear ends. The whips kept rounding them up, only to have them break away again.

"This is as hopeless as herding cats!" Jimmy Bransom called to Palmer, his whip dangling dejectedly.

Palmer spotted Lucas in the doorway of the tobacco barn. He had trained the hounds and liked to watch them work. Bunches of drying burly tobacco leaves hung from poles along the rafters behind him. During the harvest last month, Lucas's wife had driven a steel spike used to string the leaves on the stakes through the palm of her hand. She had merely wrapped the wound with a rag and kept on working. And Marge thought *she* had problems when their swimming pool pump broke.

As though an electrical switch had been thrown, the hounds headed through the gate, followed by the whips. They raced across the field toward the West Woods, one swelling and contracting mass, a cell about to divide. Palmer loosened his reins, and his gelding Colonel pranced through the gate behind them.

Alvin took a practice jump over the chicken coop in the fence, his horse's hooves thumping the wood. Someone who'd had too many stirrup cups let loose a rebel yell. Leather squeaked and metal clanked. Horses whinnied and tossed their handsome heads. A couple of riders charged across the soggy field, reining in to one side of Palmer. The cortege glided toward the skeletal woods as though in a disorderly death march behind some distant hearse.

Colonel tiptoed through the damp fescue, fighting the tight reins. Palmer sat easily in the smooth curve of the saddle, not unaware that he looked pretty good sitting straight and tall in his blue jacket, high black boots, and top hat. He inhaled deeply, pleased by the prospect of a morning of hard riding with his friends from Beulah, with whom he'd grown up and gone to UVA, with whom he now did business deals and attended church services, parties, weddings, and funerals. Spotting Lucas by the barn, gazing at him with that bizarre blue stare, Palmer squared his shoulders and angled Colonel to exclude Lucas from his line of vision.

Mixed in among the caws of crows and muted conversations of riders, Palmer detected Julius's howl. They'd barely started. Wasn't it too soon to have picked up a scent? He waited for Julius to recognize his mistake. Colonel tensed his muscles for the chase.

Soon Julius was joined by the rest of the pack, howling like air-raid sirens. There was no question they were in serious pursuit of something. Palmer slackened his reins and Colonel surged forward, nearly catching him off balance. They cantered toward the West Woods.

Taking the fence, Colonel careened across a carpet of leaf mold, weaving among the tree trunks like a slalom skier. Palmer lay alongside Colonel's neck as a branch swatted off his top hat.

As they paralleled the fence line, Palmer could see old man Partridge sitting by his pond, casting his fishing line into the murky water, not so much as glancing up at the racket going on in the woods beside him. Palmer had tried several times to buy Partridge's place after the man's wife died. He figured the old man might like to move into Beulah near his daughter. But each time, old man Partridge acted as though he hadn't even heard Palmer's offer.

Leaving the woods behind, he and Colonel reached the red clay rise to the plateau. Without a moment's hesitation, Colonel scrambled up it, arcing again and again like a salmon leaping upriver. Upon reaching the flat shelf up top, he broke into a gallop, throwing up a spray of red clay and staining his graceful white forelegs a burnt orange.

They had been locked up all week, Palmer in his office and Colonel in his stall. Both craved this illusion of freedom and flight. Palmer knew there were limits to his ability to play the solid citizen. These moments of folly and terror were his drug of choice. In the valley below, he caught glimpses of the streaking hounds, intent on their scent, wherever it was leading them.

Reaching the far side of the ridge, Colonel didn't so much as slow down. He plunged off the edge like a diver, nearly pitching them both forward into somersaults. Just in time his front legs locked, and he skidded down the face of the bluff, hooves plowing furrows in the sticky clay.

When they arrived in the valley, Palmer could hear other riders above him on the ridge, whooping with delight or shrieking with fear. Marge was a smart woman: this country was too precipitous for hunting. It was a miracle someone hadn't been killed yet.

Palmer heard the hounds not far ahead. They weren't sounding frustrated and bewildered, as when they'd lost the scent. But it wasn't the chilling bay of success either. It was a sound Palmer had never before heard from them. They were yipping almost like pups taken too soon from their bitch.

Palmer wove through the trees, Colonel dancing two steps sideways for every unwilling one forward. Frowning, Palmer forced the horse ahead, kicking him in the flanks as he rarely had to do. What the hell was going on?

Parting their way through a curtain of tangled grapevines, they entered a narrow clearing fenced in by bare gray saplings, ghostly sentinels, like the branches that loom up out of the mist in nightmares about moonlit midnight pursuits. Julius crouched off to one side, trembling and whimpering. The other hounds had formed a tight semicircle. They inched forward, then scooted back, whining and yelping.

The object of their hysteria was a moth-eaten red fox. It was shuddering like a baby with convulsions, palsied head bobbing. Spittle oozed from its mouth to fleck its mangy coat and the mat of dead leaves below. Its burning eyes seemed to focus on Palmer.

Grabbing his brass horn from his waistband, Palmer played the tattoo he and Lucas had worked out to signal trouble. He climbed down from Colonel. The horse shied dramatically and bolted off into the trees, where he stood with his reins tangled around one fetlock, tossing his head and rolling his eyes back to reveal the whites, like a silent movie actress.

Palmer walked over to Julius, who was shivering in spasms. A chunk was missing from his neck, and his fine fawn coat was caked with blood. Stooping to pat him, Palmer remembered buying him as a pup from a stable near Charlottesville, seduced by the shape of his head, which had promised unusual intelligence. And this promise had been fulfilled.

Looking up, he saw Lucas, mounted on his fastest mare, fighting his way through the web of tangled vines. His mare was hopping in place, reluctant to move forward. Lucas slid off her and walked over to Palmer. He studied the hound and the fox. The fox, snarling weakly, dragged itself across the clearing. With a final backward glance, it disappeared into a maze of brambles and briars.

The fox seemed to have had hypnotic powers. The mesmerized movements of the other animals continued for several moments before all hell broke loose. Horses snorted, reared and lunged. Hounds raced around the clearing, baying boldly now. The blue coats and black hats of other riders began to appear among the grey saplings.

Lucas turned to stare at Palmer with his annoying blue gaze. Palmer averted his eyes, feeling guilty. But what in God's name was he guilty of? By the time he realized that the fox should be destroyed, it was long gone.

Palmer surveyed the new milking parlor and the freshly whitewashed hay barn. Regardless of how Lucas maintained his house, Palmer insisted that the farm buildings be in mint condition, and they were. The Holsteins were lined up awaiting relief for their bulging udders. A few heads turned to look at him with eyes of melted chocolate. There was never any question which got milked when. Lucas said he always knew which cow would be through the door next.

When Palmer reached the parlor, he heard voices raised above the hiss of the machines that passed milk from the udders through cooling coils into the refrigerated tank.

"Lord, Lucas, that man is just as cold as a walk-in freezer. Don't leave you nothing but a living."

Palmer recognized Red's voice.

"Can't a small farm do nothing no more," replied Lucas.

"Not when his neighbors gang up on him."

"He helped us when we was whipped."

"Helped you? Didn't leave you no choice but to sell out. That, or turn on him, one."

As Red's words sank in, Palmer felt anger sweep over him like a blast from a furnace on a dog-day afternoon. You knocked yourself out trying to help these people, but all you harvested was resentment. He'd taken a bunch of run-down dirt farms and turned them into the best dairy operation in the state. The butterfat content of his herd's milk had broken regional records. Without him, half a dozen families would have starved to death in winter or moved to factory jobs in town. Kudzu would have buried their shacks without a trace.

Lucas appeared in the doorway. He looked like a boy, but the lines around his mouth and across his forehead showed his age. Hands stuffed in his overall pockets, he squirted a stream of tobacco juice through the gap between his front teeth. It splattered on the gravel. Turning to go back in, he spotted Palmer. His face flushed. "Howdy, Palmer. Didn't know you was out today."

"Just got here. How're you today?"

Neither looked at the other. Palmer knew his own face must still be crimson.

"Fine, I reckon." Lucas ambled over.

"Came out to see how Julius is doing." Palmer tried to sound hearty, despite feeling as though an arrow were twanging in his chest.

"I done told you this morning that he ain't doing so good."

Palmer and Lucas strolled toward the barn.

"All these modern wonder drugs will fix him up in no time flat," Palmer said.

"Seem like the spirit flowed plumb outen him after that fox ripped him up like that."

Palmer glanced at Lucas with exasperation. This was one of his typical Old Testament pronouncements.

They stopped before a cage against the barn. Inside lay Julius, head between his paws. Both men squatted and studied him. His panting was the gasp of a drowning man about to sink for good.

"Hey, Julius," called Palmer.

The dog lifted his lids to reveal watery crimson eyes. He turned toward Palmer with a plaintive whimper.

"See what I'm telling you?"

Palmer nodded. Until now he hadn't seriously entertained the possibility that Julius might not recover. "Did you tell Red and the others that we have to find that fox and make sure it's dead?"

"Yeah, I told Red. But he says he ain't helping."

"Why the hell not?"

"He says it ain't his concern." Lucas was giving Palmer his blank blue gaze.

"But it can get after his cows just as easy as ours."

"He says he ain't helping 'cause you done turned that fox crazy."

"Me? It's rabies. From bats."

Lucas shrugged. "Could be Red knows some things you don't."

THE EYE OF THE LORD

Old man Partridge places his Dixie cup of worms in the yellow plastic pail. Grabbing the handle in one hand and his fishing pole in the other, he shuffles across the meadow.

The leaves are turning to gold and purple on the oaks and poplars across the fence line. Milkweeds and wild raspberry canes are taking back this field his grandfather cleared a hundred years ago. But he's sold off the last of his heifers, so there's no point in keeping it open. His son is an executive at a GM plant near Detroit. His daughter Anna married Doc Roller and moved into town. Different ones have tried to buy him out, but he aims to end his days right here where they began.

Setting the bucket and pole on the limestone ledge by the pond, he hunkers down and plucks a worm from the dirt in the cup. It stiffens and lashes like a handled snake. With trembling fingers he struggles to work its length along his hook, recalling the way his wife struggled toward the end of her life to thread a needle and sew him on a shirt button. Finally successful, he tosses his line into the water and begins the long wait until lunchtime.

The sky is clear, and there's a warm breeze up the cove from the river. The leaves rustle in the woods like a crowd whispering secrets. It feels strange to be waiting around to discover what's going to do him in. Some tumor already spreading through his guts like poison mushrooms in leaf mold. A vein in his brain clogging up like a bathtub drain. A gun thug some dark night, searching for his money stash. The outcome isn't in doubt, but the method will be a surprise. His wife used to worry herself sick about roof falls when he was working in the mine, but here he is fishing on a rock while she lies moldering in her grave on that grassy hillside outside of town.

His line goes taut. He isn't entirely pleased to have his morning meditation interrupted. Reeling it in through the sun-struck water, he discovers a good-sized bluegill. It writhes in midair, rainbow scales flashing like mica. Carefully, he removes the hook from the torn mouth. The worm has vanished, probably down the fish's gullet. He lays the fish on the rock, where it flops feebly.

Climbing down to the red clay bank, the old man fills his bucket with water. He places the fish in the bucket, where it settles right down, either resigned to its fate or believing it's escaped. He rebaits the hook with a more docile worm and casts it back into the water.

Perched on his rock, he studies his free hand as though he's never seen it before. Thick blue veins meander through a field of liver spots. The finger joints are burled like mulberry branches. This is the same hand that picked a banjo at the barn dances where his future wife, then sixteen years old, first started to notice him. This hand held hers while they were courting. It caught their babies' heads as they fought their way out of her womb in the spool bed up at the house. This hand cut tobacco, shoveled coal, and steadied a rifle to shoot coons from treetops. Now this hand trembles as it baits a fishhook. What's going to become of him?

The shelf of limestone where he's sitting feels as comforting as a longtime friend. He's always come here when he's needed to be alone—as a son in a crowded household, as a father of unruly children, and now as an old man alone in the face of death, his wife's already accomplished and his own pending.

His fingers trace the familiar fossils of tiny marine creatures that etch the powdery limestone. A county agent told him one time that the ledge used to be a reef on the floor of an inland sea many an eon ago.

One afternoon toward the end, his wife lay sweating and moaning in that same spool bed where they had made their babies and seen them born. The preacher stopped by in his finned yellow Pontiac. After praying a spell with the dying woman, the preacher informed him that she was in spiritual labor, giving birth to her immortal soul.

"The eye of our Lord is looking down on us from heaven right now," he insisted, tightening the rhinestone cross on the clasp of his bolero tie. "Not the foot of an ant moves but what the good Lord knows it and wills it so."

Chewing on this as the Pontiac shuddered back down the dirt driveway, the old man stood on the front porch while the pond reflected the scarlet sunset. It looked like the lake of molten brimstone, ready for suffering sinners, which the preachers always carried on about at revivals. He realized that hell wasn't waiting in some future state. It was going on right here and now in his very own house. Yet the only sin his wife had ever committed was learning that a neighbor was puny too late to send him a pie. So why was the Lord punishing her worse than any common murderer, who at least got an injection to end his misery fast?

Feeling another tug at his line, the old man reels in a second bluegill. It's been so long since someone fished this pond that it's now overstocked. The notion of fresh bluegill fried up in butter isn't too hard to take. As he tosses his line back into the water, he asks himself if maybe the preacher wasn't right that day after all: it was at least possible that a Lord who could turn watery wastes into solid rock ledges could extract the immortal soul from his wife's body and transform it into an angel.

A faint meow reaches him from the pasture. Turning his head, he spots the tabby cat picking her way through the timothy. She turned up outside his house one day last month, bawling like a newborn, but leaping away into the woods each time he opened the door. He left a bowl of meat scraps and soured milk outside that night. In the morning the bowl was empty. Putting out scraps for the wild kitten soon became part of his daily routine.

Eventually the cat, bigger every day now that she was getting fed, started to hang around the yard when he was splitting kindling. She'd stalk the chickens as they pecked for grubs in the dirt. One afternoon she sneaked over to rub against his overall leg, dashing away when he bent to pet her.

On warm days he often left his front door open. Sometimes she lurked on the threshold, eying the living room with curiosity, so he named her Curious.

One morning he moved Curious's bowl from the porch to a spot alongside the woodstove. After several hours of studying the bowl from the doorway, she raced in, gulped down the food, and raced back out, vanishing into the woods for the next couple of days.

In due time, Curious ate by the stove every day. One cool morning he shut the door without thinking. When she noticed, she began to yowl like her heart had plumb broke. So he opened it. Once she learned that he would open it whenever she wanted, she relaxed. Now she lay in his lap in the armchair all evening and slept in his bed each night, as cuddlesome as his children had been when they were chubby little infants in flannel blankets.

The cat rubs against the old man's back, purring like there's no tomorrow. Then she discovers the yellow plastic pail. Looking into it, she watches the bluegills floating in the water. She lifts one paw and flexes her claws.

"Curious, you leave them fish alone now, hear?" mutters the old man. "Them's our lunch."

She stares at him. Sitting down a foot from the bucket, she wraps her tawny tail around her white feet, the picture of innocence. From time to time she glances at the bucket with narrowed eyes. Then she washes her face with one paw, pretending that fish don't interest her in the least.

A small oval cloud the shape of a milkweed pod appears overhead. The breeze has died down, so it just sits there. The center is thinner than the rim, and it looks like a milky blue iris with no pupil, an eyeball dimmed like his own by cataracts. The old man imagines it's the eye of the Lord, peering down at him, checking up on him, trying to work out how to finish him off.

Curious rises to a crouch and stays there for a good while, still as a stone statue. All of a sudden she springs off the rock into the meadow. She pounces. She seizes something in her teeth and shakes it. She hurls it into the air.

The old man sees that it's a baby field mouse, pale and blind and helpless. "Bad cat!" he shouts hoarsely. "Stop that!" Then he glimpses the bluegills gasping in his yellow pail and realizes that he's one to talk.

Overhead a hawk shrieks. Looking up, the old man spots the giant bird, which seems to emerge like an avenging arrow from the eye of the Lord. Its wing tips fringe the blue of the sky as it circles up above. Its shadow passes over the cat, which is still intent on torturing that little mouse. The hawk drifts on an updraft, wings not moving, soaring down closer and closer.

Then the hawk drops like a stone from the sky. It swoops down on the cat and seizes her with its talons. She hisses and flails her front claws. The hawk lifts off, carrying the writhing and spitting cat. They spiral up toward that strange oval cloud.

In midair the pair struggle, both suspended from the hawk's outstretched wings, like a trapeze catch gone wrong.

The cat howls. The hawk screams. Its wings flail like a revival tent in a windstorm. The two somersault. Still interlocked, they tumble toward the earth. They crash on a limestone ledge farther down the shore.

Securing his fishing pole beneath some rocks, the old man gets to his feet and hobbles along the shoreline. When he reaches the ragged bundle, he discovers that one multi-hued wing covers both creatures like a fringed feather shroud. He waits for one or the other to stir.

Finally he pokes the wing with the toe of his work shoe. No response. He squats and shifts aside the stiffening wing. Both bird and cat are dead, eyes open but without light. The white breast of each is soaked in blood. The hawk's claws are buried in the cat's chest. The cat's teeth are sunk in the hawk's throat.

The old man studies the scene for a long time, trying to make some sense of it. He looks up at that oval cloud. Then he looks down at its reflection on the glass surface of the pond.

He's never been one to criticize. He didn't smite his children nor hardly even raise his voice at them. He just tried to show them through his own actions how to do right by others.

Limping back to his pole, he reels in his line. He unhooks the worm and puts it back in the Dixie cup. One at a time he removes the bluegills from the bucket and places them in the pond. As they wiggle away into the deep, he offers them a silent apology. He never meant to ruin their morning. He'd just wanted an excuse to set a while on his favorite rock.

Crossing the field, the old man stops to empty the worms back into the patch of dirt he dug them from. As he glances up at that milky oval cloud still hovering above the pond, he wonders if the preacher would call it a sin for a mortal man to try to set a good example for his Lord.

GRASSY TOP

"Well, well," said Rachel, studying the man before her on the sidewalk outside Mayfair's. Even in khakis and a sports shirt, Thomas looked as stiff as though buttoned into a three-piece suit. His auburn hair was carefully styled, and he was wearing the green-tinted contacts that had always made his eyes look like an alien's.

He provided a startling contrast to the men Rachel knew in New York, faux revolutionaries who dressed in clothes scrounged from dust bins in back alleys. Bushy hair and full beards concealed most of their faces, just like the mountain men who lived up in the coves near Big Lick. Sometimes Peter wore a blue bandana tied low over his forehead like a pirate.

Thomas was eying Rachel's sandals, jeans, and tee shirt with distaste. But she was wearing this outfit on purpose, to notify her family and former friends and neighbors that she was no longer who they thought she was—even if she couldn't say exactly who she was instead.

"I scarcely recognized you," said Thomas.

Rachel smiled. He used to get annoyed when her shirtwaist was wrinkled, even if the wrinkles were the result of his own backseat groping.

Holding Thomas's hand was a boy three or four years old. The jade-eyed teenager Rachel used to love was a step midway between this sturdy adult and the slender boy by his side. It was like seeing the life cycle of a horse, from colt to stallion.

"Your son?" asked Rachel.

"My oldest. Will, this is a friend of Daddy's from a long time ago. Is this your daughter?"

Rachel nodded, smiling down at Molly.

"She must look like her father?"

"Yes, that's true. Fortunately for her!"

Thomas said he was managing the men's department at Mayfair's and hoped to open his own clothing store soon. Rachel remembered summer evenings strolling around town gazing into display windows as Thomas lectured her on brands of ties and shoes. Rachel also remembered the co-ed from State he had married. He wrote Rachel at Barnard to say that he was pinned to someone named Patty and wouldn't be writing again. Rachel had lain in bed for two weeks, reading each James Bond novel three times. She ended up in the infirmary with pneumonia, and in the dean's office on academic probation.

Rachel tried to describe Peter—a Marxist filmmaker who professed contempt for clothes, cars, the decoration of houses. Rachel's cure for her heartache had entailed choosing a successor who ridiculed everything Thomas valued. And it had worked for a while.

"Peter and I are separated at the moment," she added.

"Oh, I'm sorry."

"Thanks, but it's actually a relief."

"A relief?"

Rachel tried to think how to explain to someone who apparently enjoyed the institution of marriage that it struck both Peter and her as unworkable. "Once you've tasted chocolate creams," she finally said, "it's hard to settle for gumdrops."

Thomas smiled, and Rachel wondered if he thought she was referring to him as a chocolate cream. But she had meant to refer to that aspect of any relationship before the routines of life dragged you down.

"How about you and Molly double-dating for lunch with Will and me? I know a hot-dog stand with a view."

His dark blue Buick Electra had a dashboard as complicated as the instrument panel on a 747. He had always loathed his orange VW bug. But since he had been putting himself through college at the time, it was all he could afford. As they drove down the highway out of town, Thomas caught her up on their old friends, several of whom now lived in ranch houses in nearby developments with high school or college sweethearts and lots of children. They seemed to be living well-ordered lives. Especially in contrast to Rachel's current quagmire.

They turned off the main road and began to climb. Recognizing where they were headed, Rachel looked over at Thomas as he chatted away in his soft mountain drawl. Apparently he didn't remember.

Land was falling away on either hand as the car ascended the mountain. The children in the back seat, fast friends by now, squealed as the vehicle rounded a curve and they spotted buzzards circling in the air below them.

The paved parking lot held a dozen cars. Where an evergreen clump had stood was a souvenir stand. Rachel wondered how it was possible that Thomas didn't remember. She remembered every blade of grass.

Thomas helped the children out the rear door. They raced to the stand. Thomas and Rachel strolled after them, neighboring mountains spread out at their feet like bright green nubs on a chenille bedspread.

"Did you ever see such a view?" asked Thomas.

"Yes."

"Oh, that's right." He laughed. "You lived here for eighteen years. You must have been up here lots of times."

"Yes."

"What?" he asked, finally noticing her bewildered expression.

"I guess you've forgotten."

"Forgotten what?"

Rachel shrugged, reminding herself that something that was significant for one person wasn't necessarily so for someone else.

Thomas stopped walking. "Oh no. How stupid of me. I'm really sorry."

"Never mind. It's interesting to see what's happened to the poor old place. Parking lots and postcards, huh?"

The children were waving pennants that read "Visit Grassy Top, North Carolina." On a display shelf were dinner plates with the mountain and its name painted in the center.

Thomas bought sodas and hot dogs, and they hiked the gravel path to the top of the mountain. He kept glancing at Rachel over the heads of their children. He always used to look at her like that—with anxiety. He had been three years older: Was she too young for his fraternity parties? For alcohol? Were his friends' crude jokes embarrassing her?

The mountaintop was above the tree line. In the middle was the bald—a level field matted with coarse alpine grasses. The sides sloped off gently into stands of evergreens below. The bald was fenced in now with chain link, like a school playground. Other visitors were standing outside the fence. The gate wasn't locked, though, so Rachel, Thomas, and the children settled inside on the grassy plateau for their picnic. The others looked on, as though at a museum exhibit of Homo Sapiens Feeding.

Rachel realized that this spot was where Thomas had spread his old olive army blanket that sunny midsummer afternoon. The VW was smoking, having barely made it up what was then a rutted Jeep track. The only visitors in those days had been lovers with sturdy cars and a desire for privacy. You could hear any approaching car while it was still miles away.

Rachel had lain there in the sun, inspecting the tiny purple petal at the heart of a Queen Anne's lace, trying to fathom the meaning of what they were about to do. Thomas folded their clothes with annoying precision. She remembered wishing that just once he would throw himself into something without planning it to death. For months they had necked in his VW, but never before in the light of day. Much less on top of the tallest mountain in the state, in full view of low-flying aircraft and circling birds of prey.

Thomas kept giving her solicitous looks, the way a marauding cat will take time out to pat its prey with sheathed claws. But he was supposed to be the experienced one, so why did he keep looking to her for reassurance?

Afterwards, as the sun sank toward the horizon, bathing the bald in tones of gold, Thomas jumped to his feet and yelled, "I love you, Rachel!" They waited for an echo, but there was no barrier high enough to bounce the words back to them.

They rolled down the hillside in each other's arms. In the high grass at the bottom, beneath the heaving shadows of the wind-tossed pines overhead, they kissed. Then they raced back up the hill hand in hand and rolled down again. As the fields and woods below turned royal purple, they dressed, climbed into the VW, and bounced back down the mountainside toward town.

Here they sat years later, eating hot dogs with children they had spawned with other partners. Rachel glanced at Thomas, who was blotting ketchup off Will's shorts. Since he barely remembered bringing her here, it seemed unlikely he was recalling the details.

Thomas pointed out his house to the children—a faint white speck among many similar specks on an undulating carpet of housing developments, highway cloverleafs, smoking factories, and polluted orange rivers.

"It's changed," said Rachel. "And not for the better."

Thomas shrugged. "You can't fight progress."

"If you can call it progress."

"Plenty who didn't have jobs before do call it progress."

Rachel nodded, chastened. Peter would have agreed with her, but of course he had a trust fund.

The children raced off to explore the bald. They discovered that they could lie down, start rolling, and pick up a lot of speed by the time they reached the woods down below.

"Had you really forgotten?" she asked Thomas.

He blushed. "I *am* sorry."

"But then, there must have been so many."

"True."

She smiled faintly.

"Do you think you and your husband will get back together?"

"I don't know. I guess marriage wasn't what either of us had bargained on. I suppose we hadn't planned on all the tedium."

"I know what you mean."

She studied his face to see if he really did know or was just being agreeable. He had spoken fondly of his wife and their little white ranch house. His life sounded very organized, which had always been important to him.

"Because Patty and I had some fun together one night when we were drunk, here we are, faced with a lifetime of mortgage payments and college tuition." Apparently remembering he had left Rachel for Patty, he said, "Sorry."

"Would you please stop apologizing? It really doesn't matter anymore."

"Because you see where it all ends up. It could just as well have been me that you're bored with and separated from now."

They looked at each other. If they had been alone in a private place, it might have seemed natural to move into each other's arms. Rachel wondered if, once two bodies have been soldered together by passion, they call out to each other forevermore, lopped halves of a despised and discarded whole. Would this physical nostalgia develop for Peter and her too, once the pain had passed?

Will was rolling down the hill. Molly was waiting in the tall grass at the bottom. Molly had stomped down the grass to make a house with several rooms. She called, "Come see my house, Willy. Let's pretend you're the daddy bunny and I'm the mommy."

Thomas and Rachel glanced at one another.

Will raced back up the hill. He threw himself down and rolled again to the bottom.

"Come *on!*" Molly was standing over him with her hands on her hips as he lay at her feet in the grass.

Will jumped up, shaking his auburn head.

"Please? Just for a little while?"

"If you want to play with me, come roll down the hill."

"Okay," said Molly. "First, I'll roll down the hill with you. But then you have to come into my house."

"It's a deal." He held out his hand and they shook on it.

Rachel and Thomas laughed until they were lying on their backs in the grass gasping for breath. As their laughter subsided, they saw Will and Molly looming above them.

Will said, "Tell us the joke, too, Daddy."

Drying his eyes, Thomas said, "You'll hear it soon enough, son. Come on, let's go home. Mommy must be wondering where we are."

THE ARCHITECT OF UTOPIA

While Aaron's mother keened in the background, his father, a labor lawyer in Brighton Beach, announced, "If we never hear from you again, it will be too soon!" He slammed down the receiver.

Camilla's father, an internist on Sugar Hill, received the news in silence, passing the phone to her mother, who said, "I'm mailing you some money. Hide it where he can't find it because you'll be needing it." And she hung up.

Aaron and Camilla exchanged satisfied glances in the sitting room of their fifth-floor walk-up on the lower East Side. They were delighted to have flushed out four more petit bourgeois racists from behind their facades of bland liberalism.

The two were wed in the reception room of the drug rehab center where Camilla worked. She and Aaron pledged before their assembled friends to love each other until they didn't. Aaron was wearing a lace shirt bought at the Salvation Army, unbuttoned to display his pelt of curly chest hair. His sailor trousers fit his slim hips snugly, and the wide legs swirled during the folk dances following the ceremony. His hair swayed in a tangled mat like a black judge's wig.

Aaron's friends wore shearling vests, army camouflage, work shirts with bandanas knotted at the throat, faded blue jeans with matching denim jackets. The women wore ruffled peasant dresses, or bib overalls and combat boots. Everyone looked decked out for a corn husking.

Camilla watched Aaron proudly, her turbaned head thrown back, smiling defiantly. She was a handsome woman, with a clipped Afro like a Persian lamb fleece and high cheekbones from a Cherokee grandmother. Her defiance was directed at her own friends, who stood tall and silent in dashikis and African trading beads, or tailored suits with wide ties and matching pocket handkerchiefs. Their disapproval of Aaron was almost palpable in the air.

Aaron's friends, as eager to please as new puppies, tried unsuccessfully to include Camilla's friends in their circle dances and reels. This was the gulf Aaron and Camilla felt their marriage could bridge.

But theirs was a marriage of love as well as of politics, if by love is implied mutual need. Because they did need each other, even though they worked hard to deny it by relentlessly challenging each other's opinions at every opportunity. Aaron would say, "Camilla baby, I can't relate to this clinic trip of yours. You send these cats to this agency or that one, and the Man patches them up and sends them right back to what messed their minds in the first place. You want blacky to have a piece of whitey's action, but we got to, like, topple this whole fucking fascist system."

Yet Camilla's common sense kept Aaron grounded. Plus, he needed her salary to finance his filmmaking. In fact, he needed far more than that, so he borrowed from his business partner, Peter, who had a trust fund. Aaron also borrowed the wedding money Camilla's mother had sent.

Camilla, masking her Barnard accent, would reply, "I can't worry 'bout no white-boy revolution. We got hungry stomachs to fill. We got rat bites to bind up. We got ceilings falling in and no heat, and motherfuckers for landlords. These films of yours, Aaron, they ain't nothing but some sorry honkey head trip."

Yet Camilla fed on Aaron's visions of a brave new world like a baby at the breast. After a grueling day of raising bail for some falsely accused client, she would sit up far into the night listening to Aaron describe a society in which resources would be spent on the needs of the living rather than on death machines. He painted verbal tableaus of the oppressed rising up to institute an Eden on earth. Aaron saw his role as that of mythmaker for this coming transfiguration. Through his documentaries of protest marches, strikes, and police busts, he would expose the venality of the authorities and the courage of those who challenged them. He would be a trailblazer into a post-capitalist paradise.

"Can you dig this, baby?" he would pause to demand of Camilla.

"This government you want to pull down, Aaron, it's paying our rent and buying your film," she would reply wearily. But she was as hooked on these fixes of a just and righteous world as some of her clients were on heroin.

Their life together was thus titillatingly discordant. After hours of Aaron's visionary schemes, punctuated by Camilla's snide rebuttals, they would retire into each other's arms for the kind of lovemaking that blotted out any concern for the past or the future, for the color of a partner's skin or the nature of his politics. Their cramped bedroom became a cocoon of delight, off-limits to anyone else.

But this was at night. During the day they worked. They worked under a worse case of the Protestant Ethic than most captains of industry. They worked as only middle-class, college-educated radicals can work—flogged by guilt over their great good fortune. And they were not unhappy. No one in the Movement would have been so gauche as to admit to being happy while living in a decaying civilization that destroyed the weak and corrupted the strong. But they had their work, and they had each other.

Within a couple of years, Aaron and Peter had made several documentaries that won awards at underground film festivals. Since they were unable to arrange distribution, the films sat in tin cases on a bookshelf in Aaron and Camilla's bedroom.

In the meantime, comrades with whom Aaron had organized actions in obscurity for years were being quoted and photographed by *TIME Magazine* and *Newsweek* as spokesmen for the counterculture. Aaron realized that it was strictly by chance that he wasn't among them. Since he abhorred the mainstream media, he was appalled to find himself envious and resentful.

"The next thing I know," he grumbled at Peter, who had been interviewed on Walter Cronkite about the march on the Pentagon, "you'll shave off your beard to endorse aftershave during a TV football game."

Aaron's friends called Camilla an Oreo. And Camilla's friends made a point of seeing her only when Aaron was away. They made comments about the good luck of white people who could spend so much time and money on home movies when black people were being drafted and imprisoned on a genocidal scale.

"Pack up, Camilla!" commanded Aaron as he burst in the door one night. "We're splitting."

Camilla looked up from the saucepan, the contents of which she was stirring on the stovetop.

"This city is a definite down trip." Throwing off his pea jacket, he grabbed her by the shoulders. "Can you get behind this?"

He described a hill farm in Vermont, stocked like a fish hatchery with little children. "To raise children without false consciousness would be to stage a guerilla action for future generations." By the time he concluded, his non-existent farm had become a self-sufficient Third World collective.

"Aaron, honey," said Camilla, "how we gonna pay for this?"

He waved the question aside.

"It's a cop-out," said Aaron's friends.

"It's a cop-out," said Camilla's friends, in a rare instance of agreement with Aaron's friends.

A year later, on their rented farm in Vermont, Camilla gave birth to a son. Aaron named him Karl, after Karl Marx.

Their house, a sagging rust-colored colonial, was located in a grassy bowl with forested mountains rising up on all sides. Each day Camilla commuted an hour down the mountain to her job at a drug crisis center, leaving Karl with a woman named Mabel, who lived in a baby blue trailer down the road. Aaron selected Mabel because she was one of the people, her husband Cletus being an unsuccessful farmer. Camilla okayed Mabel because Mabel adored babies. Aaron couldn't tend Karl himself because he was busy rendering their homestead self-sufficient.

On summer nights after Karl was asleep, Aaron ushered Camilla around the farm, explaining what shed or crop would go where. At various spots he made love to her in the high grass like a dog marking his territory.

Aaron bought a cow, but he sometimes forgot to milk her. Often Camilla came home to a dangerously bulging udder, so she took over the milking. She also shoveled the manure on weekends. And after Aaron lectured her on the importance of controlling your food supply in a world in which you couldn't control the air you breathed or the water you drank, Camilla planted an organic garden.

Aaron picked apples from the abandoned orchard on the opposite hillside. Using an ancient rusted hand press from the barn, he made twenty gallons of cider. Since he failed to explore methods of preservation, it soon turned to vinegar. However, he got good footage of the picking and pressing. And of little Karl, the universal child, toddling across the field munching a wormy apple.

Camilla got up at six, milked the cow, fed the chickens, cooked breakfast, fed and dressed Karl, took him to Mabel's, worked all day, drove home, picked up Karl, milked the cow, weeded the garden, cooked supper, cleaned the house, did the laundry, paid the bills—and then stumbled around under the full moon for lovemaking in the meadows.

"Aaron," she finally said one night as he tried to lure her to the hayloft, "I'm worn out. I need some help."

"Help?"

Camilla realized that her own quiet competence had created this situation. "We've got to split the chores."

Aaron looked injured. "But I'm an idea man, Camilla."

"Maybe so, but your props person is losing it."

Reluctantly he agreed to help, and they limped through a couple more years, raising Karl and discovering the pleasures offered by the endlessly shifting seasons there in their grassy bowl among the majestic mountains. They watched with satisfaction on television as the war wound down, and they tried to persuade their friends to desert New York and join the coming rural revolution.

But then one day a letter from Peter arrived in their metal box by the roadside, asking for the money Aaron had borrowed to finance their move to Vermont. Peter and Rachel, one of Camilla's friends from Barnard, had separated, so Peter was supporting two households. He sounded deeply unhappy. Aaron recycled the letter in the fireplace.

A few nights later Cletus arrived on their doorstep after supper in his red plaid lumberjack shirt.

"Come in," said Aaron, shaking his hand. Aaron's blueprint for the future included organizing all the downtrodden hill farmers, who were Third World if they could only dig it. He gestured for Cletus to sit down at the kitchen table.

"Get much hay this cutting?" asked Aaron, trying to copy the dour inflections of the taciturn farmers.

"Not much. Too dry."

"Looks like rain."

"Yup."

Aaron always panicked trying to talk with Cletus, for whom silences were as important as words. Spinner of verbal visions, Aaron couldn't bear silence. Yet Cletus probably wouldn't reveal the true purpose of his visit for at least half an hour.

Once the weather, their gardens, their cows, and their children were out of the way, Cletus said, "Got to sell this farm."

Aaron looked as though a bomb had just fallen on him, but all he said was, "That so?"

"Ayup."

"How come?"

"Need money."

"How much?"

"This developer's offered me a hundred thousand."

Aaron paled. "You'll be a rich cat, Cletus."

"Nope. Debts."

"Selling right away?"

"Ayup."

Message delivered, Cletus departed. Aaron sat at the kitchen table, pony-tailed head in his hands. "Do you think we could get a mortgage to buy this place?" he asked Camilla, who was washing the dishes.

She snorted. "On my salary? With your debts?"

Aaron launched into a condemnation of private property, the international banking conspiracy, and the military-industrial complex.

"That may be," said Camilla in a jaded voice. "I don't know. But I do know that you got to get yourself a job. 'Cause I ain't paying your debts, Aaron. I can't hardly pay the rent." She was almost as surprised as Aaron to hear herself say this.

Aaron said nothing. He had thought they both regarded him as a skilled architect of utopia, rather than an unemployed deadbeat.

The next week he looked for jobs. But filmmaking wasn't in demand in rural Vermont. Although he had the training to be a commercial photographer, he refused to sell out by making studio portraits or shooting weddings and anniversaries.

A second letter, frantic and accusatory, arrived from Peter. When Aaron had taken the money, he had assumed it was a gift. Peter had a trust fund, and he didn't. The trust fund included dividends from Dow Chemical, who produced napalm. They had to be laundered by investment in socially progressive projects like the Third World Collective. Money was merely a concept. Those who received it had an obligation to share it. Those who borrowed it served the vital function of keeping it in circulation. Aaron was distressed by Peter's sudden revelation that he possessed an accountant mentality. How could you know someone so long and so well yet never realize that he was actually ruling class in his attitudes as well as in his origins? Nevertheless, something had to be done about this enraged letter.

Aaron was gone for several days. When he finally strode back into the house, Camilla looked up from the couch, relieved. He whisked out a wad of bills and tossed it on the floor. Karl was napping upstairs, so he pushed her down on the rug and climbed on top of her. She watched in disbelief at the transformation of their tender and whimsical lovemaking into a crude grappling fueled by resentment.

"Drug dealing?" gasped Camilla as she lay on the carpet afterwards.

"Yes, drug dealing," he said, mimicking her shocked voice. "Pushing."

"*Drug* dealing?"

"What do you want from me, woman? You told me to earn some money, so here it is." He ruffled the bills in her face.

Camilla sighed. "You don't see anything absurd about the fact that I spend all day trying to get people *off* drugs?"

"I'm setting you up with clients, baby. You need me. You should thank me."

Camilla studied him. "Parasites like you we could do without forever."

"Yeah, like *you* aren't leeching off the system yourself!"

He jumped up, dressed, and headed out the door.

When Aaron stormed back into the kitchen a week later, Karl was drumming on the tabletop with two asparagus spears.

Aaron announced, "Okay, Camilla. You'll no doubt be pleased to hear that I've stopped dealing."

Camilla said nothing. She was pleased. But now Aaron would have no money for his debts, to say nothing of a down payment on the farm. Finally she replied, "Aaron, if you're staying here, you're splitting the chores and you're finding a steady job. I pay the rent. I decide who lives here."

Aaron sulked and moaned, but he began pumping gas in the village. He cooked, cleaned, milked, weeded, and tended Karl. But he was deeply demoralized. If a brave new world was under construction somewhere, he was no longer one of its draughtsmen. He was a service station attendant. He turned his back on Camilla in bed and stopped dragging her around the fields at night. His harangues to his New York friends about moving to Vermont ceased.

Surveyors appeared in the meadows, and men in hard hats with sheaves of drawings. Offers were pending. Cletus reported that he was trying to figure out how not to sell, but things looked bad.

Aaron cut his ponytail, shaved his beard, and dressed in a sport coat and tie. He visited banks in Burlington, hoping that buying the house and a small piece of the land might tide Cletus over. He opened a money market account with T. Rowe Price.

Who was this shorn man discussing interest rates and closing fees, wondered Camilla one evening as they ate linguini primavera at the kitchen table. Not the audacious revolutionary who had inspired in her such ardor in the present and such faith in the future. She studied him with a faint ironic smile.

Aaron, aware of her irony, glared back. What in God's name did she want from him—guns or butter? Because he couldn't do both at once.

The next night Aaron didn't come home for the first time since he had stopped dealing. Camilla did his chores. He wasn't there the following two days either. The owner of the gas station phoned to inform him that he was fired.

After five more days he swaggered in, beard resprouting. Camilla looked up from the scramble of bills on her desk. He flopped down on the couch.

Voice shaking, she asked, "Aaron, where the fuck have you been?"

He smiled, glad she had asked. "Balling another woman."

A wave of nausea swept over Camilla. To regard each other as property was bourgeois. If she had wanted another man, she would have expected to have one without recriminations. The point was, she hadn't *wanted* one.

"Oh?" she said, feigning indifference.

"I'd like you to meet her sometime."

"Why would I possibly want to meet her?"

"You might learn something."

"I might learn something," she echoed.

"Camilla, don't you see what you've become? A middle-class career woman. You're whiter now than I am."

Camilla looked at him helplessly.

"This woman, she's something else. No hassles. And hassles are all you and I have had for months. You're bringing me down with your chores and schedules and jobs. I need a woman who can inspire me." He smiled, picturing his new muse.

"Where does she live?"

"In a commune near Trowbridge. This nuclear family trip of ours has become a total down trip. You can see that too, can't you?"

"Does she have children?" Camilla asked pointedly.

"What would a woman like her do with children? She's a free spirit. She comes and goes as she pleases."

"Last I heard, raising children was the ultimate in revolution." Camilla propped her chin on her fist and gazed at this man whom she had loved enough to abandon her entire prior life, defying and disappointing her parents and all her friends. What had happened to their rich and sustaining love?

For supper that night Camilla served a cabbage casserole. She took a bite. "This isn't hot enough, is it?" She was carefully avoiding the topic of what Aaron intended to do next.

"It's fine."

"No, it's lukewarm."

"It's great. Don't sweat it."

"Let's face it, Aaron: This cabbage is fucking freezing."

"Well, it could be a little hotter," agreed Aaron.

Camilla burst into tears. "You're always criticizing me. Nothing I ever do is right."

"Camilla, you're driving me crazy," he said in a low voice.

"I'm driving *you* crazy?" She jumped to her feet, picked up the casserole, and turned it upside down on his head like a pottery helmet. Its contents spread all over his face and shoulders.

Once his shock subsided, Aaron threw the dish to the floor, where it shattered. He leapt up, drew back his fist, and planted it in her stomach.

Karl started whimpering. He scrambled down from his chair and hid under the table.

Aaron picked cabbage off his work shirt and dropped the leaves on Camilla, who sat on the floor hiccoughing with sobs. Karl peeked out from behind a chair.

Stomping upstairs, Aaron changed, letting his cheese-coated shirt and jeans remain on the floor where they fell. He packed a knapsack and departed.

After a couple of weeks, Cletus informed Camilla that the land had been sold and they had to be out in two months. She had no idea where to go or what to do. For starters, she sold the cow and chickens to a lawyer at Legal Aid in town.

Every night after his bedtime story Karl asked, "Where's my daddy?"

She would reply, "I don't know, darling."

"Is he coming home soon?"

"I hope so."

Camilla started remembering the things about Aaron that she loved best: In winter he would pull Karl on a sled to the top of the tallest hill and they would careen back down, both shouting all the way. In summer he and Karl would jump from the highest rocks at the swimming hole, sunlight glistening off their bodies.

Her future stretched before her like a barren tundra. She couldn't imagine loving another man, and her sex life seemed a closed book. She stopped eating and lost weight, intent on destroying this body that had given them both so much pleasure. Karl was the only thing that kept her from opening a vein in the shower. Even so, she read up on which vein to open, and she designated Rachel in New York as Karl's guardian.

But as the days of Aaron's absence passed, so did the worst of Camilla's anguish. Eventually she was getting through entire hours without once thinking of him. And then one night, alone in bed, with moths fluttering against the screens and eerie night birds calling from the forest, she managed to envision a utopia of her own: Karl and herself on a sunny Caribbean island, dashing in and out of the salty turquoise sea. Or back in New York, surrounded by her old friends, in a neighborhood with a playground and playmates for Karl.

The next morning Aaron phoned. Camilla went limp at the sound of his familiar voice and collapsed into an armchair. He had moved into the commune with his new woman and was blissfully happy. Could he see Karl that afternoon?

Camilla replied that she and Karl were getting along just fine, that he could of course see Karl, who was going to Mabel's son's birthday party. Would Aaron like to take him?

"A *birthday* party? How boring."

"So don't take him."

"No, I'll take him. But that doesn't mean I have to enjoy it."

"If you take him, you keep your mouth shut. Karl's been looking forward to this party all week."

When Aaron walked through the door, Karl ran to him and threw his arms around Aaron's knees. Aaron and Camilla nodded coolly. Aaron didn't comment on her gauntness. She didn't comment on his eyes, which were ringed with blue-black from lack of sleep, whether from anxiety or from nightlong lovemaking she didn't care to know. Aaron swept Karl up to the ceiling and then carried him out to the car on his hip. Camilla stood waving in the doorway, wondering if she would ever see them again.

Mabel later reported to Camilla that when she served the children cake from the grocery store and Sealtest ice cream, Aaron lectured them all on white sugar, rotting teeth, junk food, chemical additives, and corrupt corporate food conglomerates. Afterwards, Karl wouldn't even look at the cake or ice cream. The other children gobbled theirs, with fearful glances at Aaron.

One of the presents was finger puppets. The children planned a performance for the adults. Karl's puppet was a king. Aaron leapt up and delivered a tirade about greedy royal families who oppress and exploit Third World people like Mabel and Cletus. Karl threw down his puppet and began to cry.

When Aaron returned Karl, Aaron lingered at the door, chatting about what possessions he would take now and what he'd come back for later. His things: tin film cases, an ebony fertility idol from his Peace Corps stint in Africa, an etched brass tray from his trip to India in search of a guru, pieces of coral from beachcombing in Fiji.

As he talked, Camilla studied him and wondered why he didn't just go ahead and leave. Presumably, this collapse of all their dreams and ideals was as painful for him as it was for her. A bulldozer was roaring in the meadow, hacking a wound-like road across what was to have been the communal playing field for their Third World Collective.

Finally Aaron said, "Look, Camilla, like, I mean…I don't know, man, I guess I need you."

She studied him for a long time. "I'm not surprised," she eventually replied. "I'm just not sure I need *you* anymore."

ENCOUNTER

The conversations in the crowded cafe were melding into a drone, as when honeybees swarmed the locust trees in Rachel's front yard in Vermont each summer. She sat alone at a pedestal table, twirling her half-empty glass of Burgundy by its stem and watching pedestrians drift by the tall windows like fish in an aquarium. When spring came to Vermont, melting snow and chunks of ice crashed through mountain gorges. Thawing fields turned to seas of mud. The south wall of her stone farmhouse would be covered with clusters of sluggish wasps and flies.

Here in Montreal, though, the thaw occurred in the hearts of the inhabitants. Their pastel clothing dazzled after the browns and blacks of deep winter. And the passersby were dawdling, with open, friendly faces, rather than scurrying along hunched over against the cold.

A navy canvas baby carriage rolled up. The mother, in white patent-leather boots and a cape the color of key lime pie, waved to people sitting behind Rachel. The father, a swarthy man with chestnut eyes and a Fu Manchu moustache, beamed. With an apologetic grimace to Rachel, the mother turned the carriage so her friends could see the baby. The father tilted the baby forward, one hand cradling the head and neck. The infant was wrapped in a yellow crocheted blanket. The expression was startled. The arms flailed and the tiny hands opened and closed convulsively, as though waving. The parents, their friends, and Rachel herself laughed.

The father lowered the baby and tucked in the blanket. Then he put his arm around his wife's waist and drew her to him in a gesture that excluded everyone else. Rachel felt a stab of envy. This was how she had assumed life would be for Peter and herself—an amble through perpetual spring, hand in hand with their children, forever bathed in sunlight.

But instead she and Peter separated when Molly was three, and she took Molly back home to North Carolina for solace. Then Peter persuaded her to try again, moving with him to Vermont. According to Peter, the entire state was roiling with exhausted anti-war activists, who were reclaiming abandoned farms and constructing a new world order. Peter intended to film this gentle pastoral revolution.

So Peter and Rachel bought a crumbling stone farmhouse and set to work restoring it and planting gardens. In the midst of all this rural fecundity, she found herself pregnant. Peter was pleased. She was not. She had intended to earn her master's degree in counseling at the University of Vermont once Molly entered school, and to open a practice in Burlington.

Rachel twisted her glass so jerkily that some wine sloshed out. She blotted it with a napkin. Looking up, she saw the navy carriage retreating. The last time she, Molly, and Peter had walked hand in hand bathed in sunlight had been that late summer morning in New York. They had eaten breakfast in the kitchen of her Barnard roommate, Pam. Or rather, the others had eaten. Rachel wasn't supposed to, couldn't have anyway. She had watched Peter and Molly, with identical strawberry blond hair and sapphire eyes, hunched over their cereal bowls, eating rapidly, squirming. Rachel remembered hoping that, just as Molly looked so much like Peter, she would inherit his temperament too—would be able to act decisively rather than draining the life out of everything through ambivalence.

Pam had patted Rachel's hand, which was lying on the table like a dead fish. "There's nothing to it. It'll be over by lunch. I've had four. I went bicycle riding after the last one."

"Four what?" Molly asked.

No one answered.

"I'm four." Molly held up four fingers one after the other.

On the street Peter explained to Molly, "Mommy is going to the doctor's, and you and I are going to the zoo."

Rachel walked zombie-like, thinking in time to the slapping of her sandals on the pavement, "over by lunch, over by lunch...." Molly tugged at her hand, trying to get her to join Peter in swinging her over curbs.

The reasons had multiplied in Rachel's head like fruit flies. She hadn't wanted to bring another child into a collapsing civilization. She wanted to work her way free of her nuclear family rather than becoming more entrenched. She wanted to be Rachel, not Peter's wife or Molly's mother. She felt inadequate to the task of molding young minds. She didn't know how to raise Molly in a world inimical to high ideals and noble instincts. There had been many reasons last August.

They had warned her at the clinic, as they put her back out on the street with a bag of antibiotics, that depression set in for some women at the time their babies would have been born. She had ignored these warnings, so eager had she been to believe that her act would indeed be over by lunch.

Yet she knew, as the new mother in the lime cape vanished around the far corner, that nothing could have been different last summer, nor did she now want it to have been. She knew she was merely a victim of hormones and conditioned reflexes. She knew people did what they had to and that regrets were a waste of time. She knew she was experiencing via Molly all the joys and torments of parenthood. She knew she had other things she wanted to do. Since she knew so much, why did she feel so rotten on this sunny spring afternoon?

Three men at the next table were speaking French. They had long sideburns and full heads of graying hair. Attractive men of early middle age. Because they hadn't once glanced at her, Rachel realized how frowsy she must look. She had meant to pick up something at a deli to eat in her hotel room, so she hadn't changed out of her faded blue jeans and rugby shirt, had merely run a comb through her hair and thrown on her old navy overcoat. But once outside, she had known she couldn't return to her stuffy room on an afternoon like this. So here she sat at a terrace cafe, feeling underdressed.

Two men walking by outside stopped before the next table. They waved and made funny faces, puffing their cheeks like blowfish. The three men inside motioned for them to come share a drink.

Their table was so small that only one of the new arrivals could fit. The other pointed to a vacant chair at Rachel's table and asked her something in French. She gestured for him to sit.

There sat the five men, long legs outstretched and tangled up under the absurdly small table, talking in animated French. Rachel inspected them in their sport coats and wide ties, trying to imagine what they did for work that they would be sitting in a cafe on a Saturday afternoon wearing jackets and ties.

The waiter brought Rachel soup and salad. The man at her table asked for coffee. Rachel, not having eaten since the previous day, grabbed her fork. The man looked away from his conversation to say with a brusque nod, "*Bon appetit.*"

"*Merci,*" said Rachel, lowering her head and eating hungrily.

The man smiled and nodded approval.

Rachel, as she chewed, decided that she liked him. The hazel eyes behind his glasses lenses were amused. His dark hair was kinky and receding at the temples. His face conveyed warmth and intelligence. He looked like a professor, except for his expensive suede jacket, which was more suited to an advertising executive. She noted that her pigeonholing mechanism had started to roll. A writer relaxing after a binge of work? A truck driver back from a long haul, slicked up for his weekend off? The clues she would use to sort out

Americans conversing in English—accents, facial expressions, topics of conversation—didn't apply in Montreal.

She realized that all five men were looking at her, waiting for her to answer a question she hadn't heard. Looking up, she replied in schoolgirl French, "I'm sorry, but I don't speak French."

The five nodded to one another, suspicions confirmed.

One gestured to the man at her table and asked in English, "Did this man ask permission to sit with you?" He could have been saying, "New York City has just been bombed," and it would have come out amusing. Watching his features arrange themselves was like watching the windows on a slot machine turn up three different fruits: the doleful eyes didn't match the stern mouth, which didn't match the bulbous nose.

"Yes, he did," said Rachel, smiling. "And I gave it to him."

"Good!" the man said with primly pursed lips. "That's a good boy, Max."

Max smiled tolerantly.

They went on talking in French. Occasionally they glanced at Rachel, who wasn't sure whether they were talking to her, about her, or were just checking to make certain she wasn't understanding whatever scurrilous things they were saying. In any case, the solitude of her afternoon meal was destroyed. It seemed forced always to focus on her food, or her hands, or the wilting jonquil in the bud vase. But if she turned in Max's direction to look out the window, he addressed her, or switched the general conversation to English to include her.

"I call myself Max," he offered at one point.

"Hello, Max. I'm Rachel," she said between bites.

"You are from the States?"

"Yes. Vermont."

"You are here on holiday?"

"Sort of."

"You are enjoying your meal?"

"Yes, thanks."

"Good!"

The waiter still hadn't brought his coffee. "*Garcon!*" he called. "*Cafe, s'il vous plait.*"

"They're very busy," Rachel pointed out.

"So they are busy," he snapped. "We are all busy."

"I'm not busy," Rachel said, realizing too late that it might sound flirtatious.

"No?" He paused. "And what are you doing this afternoon, for example?" A sly look came into his eyes.

"Eating lunch at the moment," she said, trying to retract any possible overtones to her previous remark. But maybe Max too was just making polite conversation, and she was imagining that calculating look in his eyes? Here they sat, companions at a small table. She was damned if she would feign aloofness just from some neurotic fear that good manners might be misinterpreted.

"And then?" he asked.

In fact, she was doing nothing that afternoon, or the next, when she would probably return to Vermont. Let's see, she reasoned, if I say I have no plans, that leaves me no excuse if he asks me to spend time with him and I don't want to. On the other hand, why get caught up in lies just because of some female neurosis that suspects every pleasant man of having ulterior motives?

"I'm meeting friends at four thirty," she said, giving in to the neurosis.

He glanced at his watch, apparently doing some calculations of his own. Rachel looked at him coolly, waiting for his next move. It was like playing chess. Though, when she thought of it like that, she reprimanded herself: Why do I flatter myself that he wants anything more than a little human decency while we're stuck at this table together?

Max's friend leaned over, smiling cheerily, to ask, "So how are you two getting along, eh?"

Rachel looked away, annoyed. Apparently she wasn't the only one with suspicions. "Why are all of you wearing ties on a Saturday afternoon?" she asked, to change the subject.

Max fingered his handsome tie, the print of which resembled a Jackson Pollack painting, and said, "Oh, I rarely wear one. I thought I would put one on this afternoon to cheer myself up. Do you like it?"

"Yes, it's gorgeous." Rachel filed away in his personnel folder the fact that he rarely wore ties.

"You are married?" Max pointed to her wedding band.

"Yes. I have a daughter."

"You are missing them?"

"Actually I'm here to get away from them."

"Ah." He nodded. "You and your husband no longer enjoy each other?"

"Oh, but we do. It's just that...." She hesitated, trying to think how to explain complex matters in basic English to a total stranger; how to discuss the superhuman virtues required to keep marriage calm and pleasant without its becoming dull, virtues that she and Peter apparently lacked. In the beginning they had fought and yelled and wept—and dragged each other off to bed for hours of steamy sex. Now they split the housework and the care of Molly. They were kind to each other. They made love like old pals. In short, they had mellowed into middle age while still in their twenties. They were currently examining a concept new to both—that it was their duty to follow through on situations they had gotten themselves and others into. This notion appealed to neither. But when Rachel returned home, they would either have to separate again, or accept a marriage devoid of passion, because the passion had fled, this time apparently gone for good.

"Are you married?" she asked Max.

"Alas, no. I have not the time. Nor the woman."

It seemed unlikely then that Rachel could make him understand. "I love my husband and my child. I just don't like marriage or motherhood."

"I see," he said with a frown that indicated he didn't see. They sat in silence, Rachel eating salad and Max stirring his coffee. The other table kept erupting in laughter. Pastel blurs continued to drift by outside.

"When do you leave?" Max asked.

Let's see, reasoned Rachel, remembering they were conceivably locked in a game of wits. If I say I'm staying two more days, I won't have an excuse for not seeing him. But maybe I want to see him. But who says he wants to see me? Her instincts felt awry in this alien culture. "Tomorrow morning."

"Rachel, would you like to come with me this afternoon?"

The first question was answered. He wanted more than polite conversation. The next question was *what* more. "I have to meet friends at four thirty," she reminded him, trying to recall what time she had given in her initial lie. Her bad memory was what usually kept her honest.

"It is only three now."

"Only three?"

"I have to take some things to the laundry. Then we could have a swim in the pool in my apartment building. You could phone your friends to say you will be late."

A swimming pool in his apartment building? Most likely he wasn't a truck driver or a writer. What was he? "But I don't have a suit," she said.

"No suit?"

"Why would I bring a bathing suit to Montreal in April?"

He thought this over. "There is a sauna in my building also."

He wanted her to swim with him? He wanted company in the sauna? Why not? Just because almost every other heterosexual man she had ever met had ultimately wanted sex was no reason to assume Max did too. But it seemed important to know what he wanted so she could decide how to answer. The idea of drinking and talking with him was appealing. She dreaded returning to her room and confronting her same old boring turmoil about marriage and motherhood, life and love. She knew she was torturing Peter with her inability either to call it off or to make a real stab at working things out. Sometimes she wondered if she wanted to pursue a degree in psychology merely in order to figure out herself.

But spending the remainder of the afternoon in bed with Max was a decision of a different magnitude. It might be naive at her age to accept a sauna, or even a drink, if she weren't open to sex. She was familiar with the scenes that could ensue. She could almost hear Max saying, "But why did you agree to come with me to do my laundry if you did not intend to go to bed with me?" But maybe Max didn't know what he wanted either. Maybe, like her, he was just curious to see what might develop.

Looking him in the eye, Rachel asked, "Why?"

"Why what?"

His friend leaned over and patted Max on the shoulder. He said to Rachel with a reassuring nod, "You like his tie. That's a very nice beginning."

Rachel and Max glared at him.

"Why do you want me to come to your apartment?" asked Rachel *sotto voce*. The virtue of his basic English and her nonexistent French was that they had to come directly to the point. She had no intention of being strangled with a Jackson Pollack necktie in a Montreal high-rise by some charming psychopath.

"I find you…en-ter-resanting."

"You find me what?"

"En-ter-resanting." He whipped out a ballpoint pen and wrote the word on his bill.

"Oh. Interesting."

"You don't understand my English?"

"Your English is fine. Much better than my French, I assure you."

"I would like to talk some more about your marriage that makes you so unhappy."

Rachel looked at him warily.

"Also you excite me."

Rachel choked on her soup. Putting her fingertips to her chest, she said, "Me?"

"Listen to me. I am a passionate person. I am also an instinctive person. I am Saggitare. And I know instinctivement that you are passionate also."

"Me?" Rachel was astonished that anyone would actually say such things. But she was relieved to have question number two answered: Max wanted more than a sauna companion. Question number three: Did *she* want more than a sauna? There was sex, and there was sex. The one word had to serve for different experiences. Sex with Peter now was an expression of affection. Sex with Max would hopefully be an hour of uncomplicated lust.

The last time she had experienced serious lust had been last summer. Molly was playing at a friend's house, so she and Peter wrestled, tackled, and groped in the woods behind their house. In the course of it all, she forgot her diaphragm and ended up pregnant. But given her diaphragm, an urban version of that afternoon wouldn't be entirely unwelcome.

"Yes, you." Max reached under the table for her knee and grabbed his friend's hand instead.

His friend looked away from his conversation, surprised. Picking up Max's hand, he kissed it, saying, "Not here, Maxie. Not in front of your new young lady friend."

Max snatched his hand away and returned it to his lap. "Listen to me, Rachel. I am a physician. I see every day the wrecks women make of themselves by inhibiting their animal drives."

Doctors, registered Rachel. Of course. She had passed a large brick hospital one block over.

"But you must see all you want of women during office hours," said Rachel. What would it be like to make love with a doctor? Would he be so jaded by women's bodies that it would resemble a pelvic exam? Or with his superior knowledge of anatomy, would he know all kinds of exotic tricks?

"I work very hard, Rachel. On my time off I like to relax with a beautiful and en-ter-ressanting woman. Please come with me this afternoon. It will be good for us both."

Rachel was touched. Why all these games between men and women? Why not just an honest declaration of motives? It was far more moving to her than a courtship of bad wine and empty promises. His candor was a compliment to her intelligence. She was so flattered that she decided to accept. Why not a pleasant tussle with this attractive man? If Peter ever found out, he probably wouldn't care more than briefly. They no longer expected to be the whole world to each other. Why had she wasted so much time?

"All right," she said. "Sure. Why not?"

He looked surprised, and not entirely pleased. After a moment he said, "Fine. It is settled, then. You will come with me."

Rachel began to feel uneasy. She kept struggling to abandon herself to the idea of a lost afternoon of lust. One problem was that her diaphragm with its five-percent failure rate was in her hotel room. Although she had had no idea she might use it, she had vowed after her abortion never to be without it again. But wearing it each time she went out the door had seemed to carry caution too far.

Max's friend stood up, grabbing Max's arm. "Come along, my friend."

Max said with a self-conscious smile, "You go on. I will stay here to finish my coffee."

The friend looked back and forth between Max and Rachel, finally walking off with the three other men. Waving to Rachel, he called with a knowing smile, "You really must let Max show you around our lovely city."

Friends departed, Max seemed to lose interest, as though the game had been played with one eye on them. He gazed across the room in silence for a long time. Maybe he was wondering what he had gotten himself into. What would his doorman think when he brought home this scruffy young woman in faded jeans with dirty hair? Maybe he had a roommate, male or female? Maybe he had other plans for the afternoon. Maybe he was worried about whether he could "satisfy" her?

Suddenly their impromptu tryst was seeming very tense indeed. It was no good, Rachel realized. Either it would be awkward and pointless due to their lack of commitment (in which case, why bother?), or it would be intense and meaningful, its repercussions more than she cared to cope with in her current stalemate with Peter. This proposed bout of passion could no more be over by dinner than her abortion had been over by lunch.

As Rachel stared out the window at the strolling pedestrians, she envied men their tradition of brigandage and piracy. Their models from the past were vagabonds and buccaneers who took their pleasure where they found it and left women to cope with any consequences. Whereas, reviewing the history of her own sex, all she could locate were ghostly legions of martyrs, marbled with self-sacrifice like choice steaks with fat. Many men and some women, like Pam, could drift in and out of encounters. Rachel couldn't. She always got involved. She suspected it was a character flaw in a world in flux.

In short, she was unable to conjure up the frame of mind that could say, Why not a tumble with this appealing guy? A voice in her head kept saying, Sure. Why not? On the other hand, why? What's in it for you except a chance of pregnancy?

"What's in it for me?" she asked herself out loud.

Max looked shocked. "Of course, if it's a question of money...."

"I didn't mean it that way. Look, Max, I've changed my mind. I'm going back to my hotel."

"And I can come with you?"

She had meant to drop the whole thing. But this variation appealed to her. She would hold him captive in her room and interrogate him: "Doctor, tell me: How can I feel male flesh moving in me without thinking about the possible outcome?"

The reception room had been decorated with Day-Glo posters of suffragists and early birth control activists. The other patients were tired housewives, gum-chewing clerks, and co-eds with sobered fraternity men. One young girl, accompanied by her parents, clutched a teddy bear. Unlike in most waiting rooms, everyone in this one knew why all the others were there.

Afterward, they regrouped in the recovery room like an army unit after a battle. The others chatted, ate chocolate-chip cookies, drank Cokes, and devoted themselves to the task of raising their blood-sugar levels. Refusing the refreshments, Rachel lay there hoping her blood-sugar level would drop so low that her body would shut down altogether.

Rachel could imagine Max's professional comments: "My dear young woman, these feelings are not abnormal. You are afraid of another unwanted pregnancy. These feelings will pass."

But knowing her fear would pass didn't alter the dampening effect it was having on this afternoon's proposed dalliance. What wouldn't pass was a bit of hard-won wisdom: People were very different from one another. Some could embrace serendipitous situations with ease; others couldn't. A sexual interlude with Max wasn't a real possibility for her, she now saw. She didn't want marriage, but she couldn't handle casual sex. How in the world was she supposed to conduct the rest of her life?

And where did it come from, this haunting ideal, apparently unattainable for her, of the loving couple hand in hand with their cherished children? Was it conditioned into her by all those years of TV sitcoms? Or was it inherent in the female psyche to want, like the barn swallow, one mate and a nest full of fledglings? Was it a reflex that had to be stamped out, or should it be honored as embodying her finest instincts? She was damned if she knew anymore.

"I want to be alone," she said, in imitation of Greta Garbo, trying to convince herself that this was true.

"But why?"

Not feeling she could explain, she said, "I have to meet friends."

"But we have an hour and a half."

"What good is that?"

"One can make much love in an hour and a half."

"Yes, but why bother?"

"Because it would be pleasant." His enthusiasm was apparently returning now that her resistance had revived.

Looking at him coolly, she thought, Tell me, Doctor, how am I to have a pleasant time in bed with you when my associations with my body at the moment are of distrust and confusion?

"Listen to me, my dear," he said. "I cannot tell you all the horrible things that happen to women who inhibit themselves as you are doing. The groin becomes engorged. This leads to many types of disorders. You must heed your drives, for the sake of your health."

"I have all the drives I can cope with at home. But thanks for your concern."

"So this is the problem. Your husband, he is an animal. He disgusts you with men and with love."

"No." She laughed. "He's not an animal. He's very nice." She wondered how an innocent coincidence that had landed a stranger at her table could have evolved into a discussion about what was best for her groin.

"But if you like him and lovemaking with him is good, why do you escape to Montreal?"

She shrugged. "I'm in Montreal because I need to be alone. I'm flattered you want me, Max, and I find you very attractive. But I'm going back to my hotel now. Alone." She stood up.

"But why won't you come with me?" groaned Max, caring more than he had all afternoon.

As a last resort, however sentimental and dishonest, she held up her hand with her wedding band on it.

He nodded in sudden comprehension. "You've never been unfaithful to him."

She looked at him, saying nothing. That was true, but it wasn't really the issue.

Max gazed at her, amused. He took her hand and kissed her wedding band. "Well, well. I of course think you are making a big mistake. However, I salute you for your loyalty to your husband. It is a rare quality these days."

Damn him if he doesn't sound as though he really means it, thought Rachel. He had spent an hour trying to seduce her, but would have secretly scorned her if she had acquiesced.

"But what a pity," he added with a rakish smile.

"Yes, I know." Rachel smiled regretfully at the whole situation. With a wave she slipped out the door into the stream of passersby, a dark blue blob clotting the pastel flow.

WEDDING BELLES

I first suspected I was making a mistake marrying Winston when I glanced at my bridesmaids during our wedding ceremony and realized that I had slept with them all.

There had been several days of brunches, luncheons, showers, cocktail parties, and dinners, each involving many magnums of champagne. The final event was a buffet beside my godmother's swimming pool at her house outside my Connecticut hometown. That morning I had had my hair styled á la Marie Antoinette. I had also had my nails polished Pearly Pink, and my legs and bikini line waxed.

During these treatments, I kept thinking about what a lucky woman I was. Winston and I dated while he was at Harvard Law and I was working for a travel agency near the Square. He walked into the office one afternoon with a bouquet of red roses, got down on one knee, and beseeched me to marry him in rhymed couplets, while the other agents applauded and cheered and booked their clients on the wrong flights. Say what you like about Southerners; at least they're romantic.

When it was nearly time to go into my godmother's bedroom, slip on my white gown, and head for the church, I looked at the guests milling around the pool—my parents and grandparents and their friends, my friends from high school and college, Winston's relatives from Tennessee, Winston's and my friends from Cambridge, several already married with small children. Some were drunk. Others had those dopey Prozac smiles. I pictured Winston and myself in a few decades. He'd commute to a law firm on Wall Street. I'd raise our children in an expensive suburban house. He'd have affairs with airline hostesses and pick up STDs. I'd fantasize about shirtless blond stevedores on the afternoon soaps. Our children would grow up to despise our middle-class compromises, and would move to distant states. Winston and I would sit on our piece of prime real estate, unable to sell it because of capital gains taxes, boring each other to death. One would see the other through a grueling terminal illness and then check into a retirement home for a lonely, morphine-mediated demise.

Anesthetized by champagne, I stumbled toward the pool and threw myself in, destroying my hairdo and losing my contacts. When I surfaced, every woman on the patio was in a state of consternation. Unlike the men, who had no notion how much time and effort my pompadour had represented, the women grasped my symbolism. Marlene, carefully shielding her own elaborate hairdo, which featured tendrils that draped her brow like wisteria vines, waded in after me. Her purple silk caftan billowed up around her slender waist like a jellyfish tent.

As she helped me up the steps, she whispered, "Darling, it's not too late to change your mind."

But when I reached the patio, my godmother, my grandmother, and my mother grabbed me and dragged me into the bedroom. Seating me on the stool before the skirted dressing table, they blasted me with hairdryers. My mascara oozed down my cheeks like lava through the streets of Pompeii. A couple of women from Mother's bridge club joined in. Soon six older women in pastel silk suits were wielding hairdryers, a curling iron, a hot comb, rollers, and teasing combs.

"Don't worry, Dinah," my godmother assured me. "You'll be as good as new in no time flat."

In the mirror I glimpsed Marlene leaning in the doorway. Her tadpole eyebrows were knit together, and she looked bleak. Probably it was asking too much of her to be my maid of honor, considering.

The next time I spotted Marlene was in the parish hall. My grandmother, dressed in sequined blue satin that matched her hair, was cutting the ring finger off my elbow-length kid glove so Winston could pull that finger off during the ceremony and slip on the wedding band. Marlene grabbed my upper arm. Explaining to my grandmother that my plum lip liner was bleeding, she dragged me toward the bathroom.

Closing and locking the door, she studied me intently and shook her head until her tendrils swayed. "What in God's name are you doing, Dinah?"

Unable to think of an answer, I began to cry, once again messing up my eyeliner and mascara. But Marlene looked so gorgeous with highlights on her cheekbones, and apricot rouge accentuating the hollows underneath that I had often caressed with my tongue.

She started removing her long gloves, tugging on one finger after another, like milking a cow. "Please don't do this," she said, falling to her knees before me.

"It's too late."

"No, it's not." She raised my skirt, fighting her way through the layers of Belgian lace and past the whalebone hoop. Concealed beneath it all, she outmaneuvered the elastic of my garters and panties. I cradled her head against my abdomen like a late-term pregnancy. We used to think we had invented such acts on the nights we spent together in high school, at her house or mine. After double dating at the movies, we necked with our boyfriends in their cars just long enough to get ready for each other.

Someone rattled the door handle. Marlene paused. Whoever it was knocked.

"In a minute," I called.

The lock didn't hold. The door swung open. In walked Miss Chang, the organist, a timid woman with a widow's peak and dark eyes that, fortunately, swam with myopia.

"Excuse me," she murmured. "Is the bathroom free?"

"Yes."

Entering the stall, she paused to inspect me. "Are you all right?"

"Fine," I whispered.

"Your face is flushed. You look as though you might have a fever."

"I'm just nervous."

She smiled. "I'm not surprised. This is the most important day of the rest of your life."

I did my best to smile back at this remark, which must have originated in some fortune cookie from California.

Miss Chang kept flushing the toilet to conceal whatever unseemly noises she was making. Marlene and I remained perfectly still, except for Marlene's fingers. I closed my eyes and forced myself not to pant.

"Is there anything I can do?" asked Miss Chang as she patted her jet black bun in the mirror and eyed Marlene's gloves on the counter.

"Thanks, but I just need a few more minutes alone here to compose myself."

"See you in church then." She started out the door. She turned back to say, "And congratulations, dear girl! I wish you and your good-looking young man a long and happy life together!"

After the door sucked shut, I locked it more securely. Bracing my hands against it, I gave myself over to Marlene's ministrations.

Afterwards, we collapsed in the chintz armchairs. Marlene's burgundy lipstick was smeared around her mouth in a wide O like a circus clown.

"You do realize this has to be our last time?" I said gently. "After Winston and I are married, I'm going to be completely faithful to him."

"Dream on, sweetheart."
"I mean it, Marlene."
She drew deeply on her cigarette, casting me a jaded look.

The priest in his white cassock and fringed purple stole asked me if I promised to love, honor, and obey Winston until death did us part. I glanced at Marlene, standing beside me with her bouquet of mauve lilies. She arched one eyebrow ironically. Past her, arrayed along the steps to the altar, I could see my college suitemates—Barbara, Marie, and Jennifer—in mauve gowns and matching pumps. All three arched ironic eyebrows at me.

Barbara, a basketball star, had barely fit into the narrow bed in my dorm room. Our breath steamed the casement windows as we lay in each other's arms watching the full moon sparkle off the freshly fallen snow in the courtyard below.

Marie, the class valedictorian, lured me to the shingled boathouse, where she summarized the conclusions of three centuries of continental philosophers on the nature of desire. Then we lay down together on a pile of orange life jackets.

Jennifer and I used to go parking in a cornfield near campus with a bag of Big Macs and fries....

As the priest whispered instructions to Winston about the ring, I had to admit that Marlene and my college pals looked delectable with those wildflower tiaras crowning their heads. But ours had been lower chakra relationships. They were my past. Winston, standing beside me in his ascot and morning coat and slipping a platinum band on my finger, was my future.

Mark, his best man, his roommate from Amherst and Harvard Law, looked almost as glum as Marlene. His square jaw was flayed with shaving nicks. I smiled at him. He bared his straight white teeth at me like some cornered jungle beast.

Winston took a job with legal aid in Vermont. His first serious case was a class-action suit against a paper mill for polluting Lake Champlain. We bought a small Victorian cottage overlooking the bike path along the lake. From our deck we watched a steady parade of very fit adults, children, and dogs race past on foot, bike, roller blades, and cross-country skis. On the lake down below, people swept past in canoes, kayaks, sailboats, and rowing skulls. On water skis, jet skis, ice boats, wind surfers, ice skates, and snowmobiles. Vermonters were busy people. Soon Winston and I were busy too. We purchased skis, skates, running shoes, sweat suits, a canoe, matching kayaks, and a wind surfer.

We also joined a tandem bike group. Every Friday night we carbo-loaded at a pasta potluck at some member's house. The next morning the couples competed along grueling routes through verdant mountains and past crashing torrents.

The group prided itself on its cultural diversity. We had an Asian couple, an African American couple, several Jewish couples, a lesbian couple, a gay couple, and two bisexual couples who lived as a foursome and sometimes changed partners in mid-race. We were trying to recruit a Native American couple and a Hispanic couple. Our races were not unlike a fast-paced Noah's ark.

Each couple wore matching jerseys of their own design. Winston's and my logo featured two white doves beak to beak on a sky blue background. We wore them with skin-tight black shorts, molded plastic helmets, and bike shoes. I rode in front, leaning when and where Winston told me to, and pedaling my buns off. Soon we were streaking around the countryside, usually placing among the top ten. But I couldn't figure out why everyone in Vermont was in such a hurry, since there was no place to go.

For almost a year Winston and I kept so active that neither of us suspected that we were headed for trouble. I wasn't working because we were trying to have a baby and it seemed pointless to start a new job I would have to drop. Winston came from a world in which wives of professionals weren't expected to work, so it was no big deal for him that I sat at home all day long. But without a job, a baby, or the distractions of a large city, I was bored. My big question each day was how many erections I could elicit from a work-weary Winston that evening.

Plus which, I had sworn to be true to my wedding vows, not having realized what a drag this would prove. But Truth, Honor, Fidelity, and all that abstract stuff beginning with capital letters mean a lot to Southerners. It has something to do with losing the Civil War. I loved Winston, so I was trying to comply with his value system, however arcane. When Marlene came to visit, I forced her to canoe, kayak, hike, and ski. She said the only sports she liked were indoor ones, preferably horizontal. But I was determined that we would not be alone together in a small room ever again.

"You've changed," she muttered one afternoon as our canoe swiveled in circles down the lake, since she spent our voyages lolling in the bow, smoking rather than paddling. "Not for the better, I might add."

"I'm a wife now." I was struggling to keep the canoe straight, as well as myself.

"Yes, but didn't you ever hear of the Wife of Bath?"

One weekend Mark visited from Cambridge while I went to Connecticut for my grandmother's birthday. Marlene, in a sulk over my embrace of monogamy, refused to see me. So I

78

returned home Sunday noon rather than that evening as I had planned.

Mark's car was out front, as was Winston's. But they weren't in the living room or the kitchen. Nor did I hear their voices from the backyard or the den. I decided they were probably out running, skating, biking, or kayaking.

Ascending the stairs with my suitcase, I walked into our bedroom. The shades were drawn and the bed wasn't made. A breakfast tray sat on the floor. Winston usually turned into a slob when I was away.

Putting down my suitcase, I opened the blinds. Looking at the tray in the light of day, I noticed there were two mugs and two plates. Then I saw that not only was the bed unmade, but someone was in it. In fact, two people were in it.

Tiptoeing to the bed like Goldilocks, I discovered Mark and Winston, both unshaven, both sound asleep. Slowly lifting the covers, I found that they were lying naked in each other's arms, sweet and peaceful and innocent.

Backing out of the room, I closed the door. I sat on the top step, arms around my knees, brain numb. Gradually the numbness flared into fury. I had knocked myself out being faithful to a faggot!

Standing up, I marched into the guest bedroom. Grabbing my Belgian lace wedding gown from the closet, I removed it from its plastic bag. Seizing some scissors from the desk drawer, I went into a frenzy of cutting and tearing. By the time I finished, the skirt had become a hula skirt composed of streamers of lace. I laid the shredded dress across the bed.

Then I dashed downstairs to the kitchen. Wrenching open the freezer door, I grabbed the top layer of our wedding cake, which I had saved to eat on our first anniversary, only a couple of weeks away. I dumped it out of the Tupperware container. It was heart-shaped with white frosting. Its mauve roses matched my bridesmaids' dresses and pumps.

I extracted a chef's knife from the holder and plunged it into the cake. Since the cake was frozen, the blade penetrated only an inch, so I carefully pounded the knife into the cake with a marble rolling pin.

Then I phoned Marlene to tell her to heat her dildo in the microwave because I was on my way.

Winston phoned Marlene's several times. Since we were too occupied to answer, he left pathetic messages about his undying devotion, despite his behavior, which he could explain, and which didn't mean what it appeared to mean. After several days of Marlene's solace, I drove home to face the music.

Winston had festooned the living room with ragweed and goldenrod, so I immediately began to sneeze as he took me in his arms and begged forgiveness. Then he insisted on taking me in the canoe to the most atmospheric restaurant in the area, the Silver Moon Inn, on the opposite side of the lake. He refused to let me paddle.

When we reached the restaurant, an elaborate Adirondack log camp built by some robber baron at the turn of the century, he ordered a bottle of Mumm's. He even choked down a couple of my oysters, despite the fact that, since he had grown up landlocked, he loathed creatures of the sea.

"Dinah, I'll do anything to get you back," he said over an after-dinner brandy.

"You should have thought about that before you alienated me in the first place."

"Please don't say that."

"You like men and I like women. What's the point in staying married?"

He choked on his brandy. "You like women?"

Realizing too late that I had let the pussy out of the bag, I said, "Sure. Who doesn't? Women are great." I studied my plastic swizzle stick intently. It was a miniature neon pink matchlock rifle, in keeping with the revolutionary decor.

Winston stared at me in silence.

"Time to go," I announced, jumping up and heading across the deck to the dock.

Winston paddled us up the shoreline past granite cliffs and pine forests, while the luminous dusk faded into night.

"I read the other day that the Abenakis have a legend about some prehistoric sea monster that lives in this lake," I said, to divert Winston from the topic of my enthusiasm for my own sex.

"Well, even if there used to be one, it's probably dead by now, from all the crap the paper mill has been spewing into the lake for the last several decades."

"Let's hope it's dead. What would we do if it turned up right now, wanting a bedtime snack?"

As we started across the lake toward home, a lightning bolt split open the ebony sky and thunder crashed all around us like a head-on collision.

"Shit," said Winston, changing course and paddling fast for a nearby cove.

As we beached the canoe, rain began in earnest. Lightning cracked like fluorescent whips, and thunder rumbled and roared. We sat in silence under the dripping pines, both presumably wondering what to do about our sham marriage. A couple of times I nearly threw up my oysters, I felt so upset. It had been easier to accept that my husband was gay when I was lying in Marlene's arms.

The rain slackened, and the number of seconds between the lightning and the thunder increased. So we climbed back into the canoe and paddled as though pursued by panthers.

After a couple of minutes, though, a flash of lightning directly overhead nearly fried us in our aluminum canoe like bacon bits in a skillet. The hairs on my forearms stood erect.

We whirled around and headed back to shore, crawling under the trees just as the storm resumed in all its fury.

"Since we may die here tonight," said Winston, "at least tell me that you forgive me for this mess."

He sounded so miserable that I muttered, "It's okay, Winston. I forgive you."

"Do you see any hope, or should we just call it quits?"

I shrugged. Realizing he couldn't see my shrug, I said, "Maybe we could try some therapy or something. That seems to be what people up here do when they don't know what else to do."

"Okay. Let's start this week."

"If we live that long."

"We'll live that long," Winston said. "I'll get us home. Don't you worry."

I always loathed him most when he went manly on me, but that night it came in handy. He paddled as fearlessly as a Cherokee warrior, dodging lightning bolts and floating branches. When we reached the other side, he insisted on carrying the canoe to the house on his shoulders unassisted.

He hoisted the canoe off his back and set it on the rack by our rear door. As he stood there in the light through the kitchen window, fair hair sodden, soaked seersucker jacket draped across one arm, soft amber eyes sad and bewildered, I acknowledged that he and I were more alike than I had realized. We had both followed wherever love had led us, and there was apparently room in our hearts for more than one. Maybe that was why we had picked one another.

STORMY WEATHER

Lying facedown on her watermelon beach towel, Jesse tries to decide what to wear to this party by the lake that she doesn't want to go to. But since it's her own fiftieth birthday celebration, she has no choice, short of dropping dead. Still, it strikes her that if you feel like celebrating at fifty, you just don't understand what's happening.

She rolls over on her back and, propped on her elbows, glances down at her no-longer pert breasts. Gravity is winning out over centrifugal force. At fifty maybe you're entitled to accept the laws of nature and abandon the struggle for fitness?

She studies the grass around the pool, scorching in the summer sun. In the late sixties, she and Robert dragged Cybele to swimming holes all over Vermont. Naked parents smoked pot along sunstruck creek banks, while embarrassed children with names taken from natural phenomena—Forest, Coyote, Sky, Storm—concealed themselves under layers of towels.

But then Robert went suburban on her, spending their savings on this pool, which has leaked ever since. Several years ago he moved to a condo in town, leaving her to patch and bail this cracked concrete vessel alone. But a love affair with herself was the only variation she hadn't tried, and she is finding solitude soothing after the sweet and savage sex wars of her youth.

Picking up the long-handled pool brush, she begins to sweep the white bottom with long, slow strokes, pretending she's a gondolier on the Grand Canal. As she stirs up clouds of debris, she hears Thor barking in the driveway. Laying down the brush, she tiptoes to the copse of Russian olives that separates the pool area from the white gravel driveway. A car door slams.

Bent over petting Thor is Rachel, wearing a Hawaiian-print bathing suit with leg holes up to her waist. She is one of the few women Jesse knows who looks good in that style. Robert is standing beside her in baggy bathing trunks to his knees and an antique Grateful Dead tee shirt. Now that the dust has settled, Jesse is fond of them again, individually and together. But this particular birthday afternoon she prefers to assess the damage of the decades unassisted.

"She's not here," Robert decides.

"Her car's here," says Rachel.

Someone could have stopped by to pick me up, Jesse silently suggests.

"Let's knock," says Robert, starting up the driveway. The laces on his high-tops are untied and he trips.

"If she's here, she probably doesn't want to be disturbed, or else she'd have come out by now."

Jesse nods in agreement, watching Rachel straighten up. Thor, not ready for her to stop patting, licks her well-tanned calf.

"Let's leave her present by the door." Robert gestures to a package wrapped in gold foil with a wide maroon ribbon, which Rachel is holding.

"Shouldn't we take it to the party?"

"She might want to wear it tonight."

Reaching the back door, Robert rings the doorbell several times. Jesse is impressed that he doesn't walk right in. He knows the hiding spot for the key, and he still sometimes regards this house as his, since the two of them restored every square inch with hand tools. Jesse recalls sawing a ten-foot two-by-four in half lengthwise, Robert insisting that to use electricity was to support the military-industrial complex that was fuelling the war in Vietnam.

"She's not here," he concludes. "Let's take a swim." Grabbing Rachel's hand, he leads her up the slope crowned by the grove of Russian olives where Jesse is standing.

Jesse's heartbeat kicks into high gear, and a hot flash sweeps up her thighs and across her abdomen. What's the polite thing to say when your friends find you naked in the bushes hiding from them?

"I'm not sure this is such a good idea," says Rachel, pulling on Robert's hand.

No, it's not, Jesse assures her. Rachel rarely steps on her toes, whereas Robert cripples her several times a month.

"Come on. It's fine. Jesse won't mind. We're all old friends." Robert drags Rachel across the granite ledge, which is etched by glaciers to resemble a giant circulatory system.

They amble past Jesse, no more than ten feet away. She's a statue, a stone nymph, Daphne turning into a laurel tree.

Thor pads along behind, panting from the heat despite his summer crew cut. He stares at Jesse, wagging his tail. Having always believed pets are telepathic, Jesse beams him a message: "If you want supper tonight, keep walking." Thor just stands there, mouth agape, tongue lolling. Jesse frowns and grimaces, trying to look punitive. Sweat from her hot flash is trickling from her armpits down her sides. It tickles but she can't scratch.

Thor follows the merry swimmers, who are now reclining on the watermelon beach towel, backs turned toward the Russian olives. The dog collapses in the shade of the barn-board pool house, doleful eyes fixed on Jesse, nostrils twitching.

A quick dip and they'll be on their way, prays Jesse.

"A towel and her robe," muses Robert like the private investigator he has always wished he were. "She must have split in a hurry."

"Who's she seeing now?" asks Rachel.

"Nobody that I know of."

"Oh, that's right. The last time we had dinner she regaled me with the erotics of celibacy. The frisson when your eyes meet those of the postman."

Damn Rachel. She had pretended to agree that night in the restaurant by the lake that there were pleasures subtler than sex. As she struggled to crack a lobster claw, she had even suggested that sex was a sublimation of love.

Robert turns his shaggy head to smile at Rachel. Jesse spots his gold earring flashing in the sun. How is a newly appointed judge able to get away with that? Do they still wear long gray wigs? Robert has developed an unfortunate double chin that puffs up like a frog's throat when he gets pompous. The same thing happened to his belly long ago.

"Sour grapes, if you ask me," says Robert. "Do you think she still resents our being together?"

Jesse is seized with indignation. *She* is the one who left, relieved to stop spending all her free time and money on therapy. Rachel and she, Robert and she, Robert and Rachel, Rachel and her husband Peter were all doing couples therapy. The four of them did group therapy. Each did individual therapy. She and Rachel processed the dynamics of their quadrangle at their women's group and in their Multiple Relationship Group. Robert and Peter processed it with their men's group. Aging is a bore, but at least the seventies are over.

"Probably," says Rachel. "It must be hard for her to see us so happy together."

In the first place, Jesse replies, I'm confident that each of you will eventually drive the other mad. In the second place....

Realizing that she is about to blow her cover, Jesse shifts her outraged gaze to the gnarled branches of the ancient honey locusts at the foot of the hill on which the pool is perched. Her favorite hour of a summer day is underway—late afternoon before the sun begins to set, when its slanting rays lend the fence posts by the cornfield in the valley shadows ten feet long. The mountains on the far horizon are exuding a golden glow. Flecks of violet and coral on the granite outcroppings signal the conflagration soon to come. She hears the plaintive coo of a mourning dove.

The bottoms of Jesse's new shorty pajamas were damp. She had climbed down from the four-poster bed and trotted across the carpet to the bathroom. Lowering the seat her father had left up, she climbed onto the toilet. Too late, she realized she was still lying in bed, dreaming this journey across the rug.

Time after time she waved the top sheet so it billowed like a sail, trying to dry out her pajamas and the bottom sheet before her mother came in. As her mother changed the sheets she had put on fresh yesterday, the muscles in her jaws would clench and unclench like fists. Jesse didn't like to make her cross. She worried that her mother might be sick. Sometimes after her father went to his insurance office downtown, her mother put on high heels and perfume and left Jesse with Mrs. Morris next door to go to doctor appointments.

Recognizing the hopelessness of her efforts, Jesse lay perfectly still while the floating sheet settled down over her. It was a blanket of snow, and she was the Little Match Girl, frozen to death.

Coming through the window from the magnolia tree outside, Jesse heard a hollow tune like her father sometimes played on his clarinet on the back porch after supper. Her mother had been the singer with her father's band at nightclubs all over the South. A man from Hollywood took pictures of her and asked her to act in a movie, but she married Jesse's father instead. Sometimes her mother spread these photos on the kitchen table and studied them.

Once again, the strange sound floated through Jesse's window from the magnolia tree. It was a sad song with five notes—low, high, low and long, low, low. Then silence.

Rolling out from under her shroud of snow, Jesse went to the window and looked through the screen into the jungle of waxy leaves and creamy blossoms that filled her room with the same scent as the perfume her mother dabbed at her throat and wrists.

The door opened and her mother walked in. Sniffing, she threw back the covers and discovered Jesse's accident. The muscles in her jaws began to pulse. The melody out the window started up again.

"Mommy, what's that sound?"

Her mother was poking the wet spot on the bottom sheet. "It's a bird called a mourning dove. It's probably calling its mate."

"What's a mate?"

"Its partner. Its husband. Or its wife. I don't know which." With a sigh she began to remove the sheets.

"Where's its mate?"

"I don't know. Apparently the dove doesn't either. That's why it's calling."

After her mother left, Jesse searched the tangled branches for the dove. Since the sound was so ghostly, she pictured a bird version of Casper the Friendly Ghost—white, with floating wings and a smiling mouth.

The dove called again. Pursing her lips as her neighbor Daryl Morris had recently taught her, Jesse whistled the melody, hoping the dove would think that she was its mate and fly over to her windowsill. But its next call came from halfway across the yard, heading for the woods.

"...it was like walking on eggs," Robert is saying. "I never knew what was going to bug her next."

"You do realize she had serious PMS?" says Rachel. "She's less touchy now that she's nearly through menopause."

Good God, protests Jesse from the bushes. *Robert* is the one who is moody, in a perpetual funk that the nuclear arms race hasn't yet destroyed the world, as he predicted in the sixties. And *Rachel* has PMS, her emotions erupting over water spots on glasses from the dishwasher, or the surly attitude of a supermarket cashier. Rachel learned in her counseling program that it was healthy to express anger, and she hasn't shut up since. Jesse admits, however, that she herself is more mellow now—but only because she's free of those two.

Looking down, she discovers that she is standing in a patch of poison ivy. The shiny green leaves-of-three are caressing her ankles and lower calves. Venom from leaves crushed by her feet is seeping between her toes. Since Rachel and Robert are engrossed in their analysis of Jesse's personality flaws, maybe she can sneak through the undergrowth behind her down to the driveway, and escape from there to the house.

She raises a foot to step backward. Thor snaps to attention in the shade by the pool house. Panting, he struggles to his feet to come greet her. Jesse returns her foot to its cushion of oozing leaves and resumes her imitation of Daphne. With a deep sigh, Thor collapses back into the shade.

"...her fear of intimacy," Rachel is saying.

Intimacy? Intimacy! sputters Jesse. Rachel's test for intimacy involved seeing who could lie in bed longest on a weekend morning without getting bored. Using that gauge, Rachel was the Intimacy Queen. Never mind that she always jumped up immediately after lovemaking to take a shower and brush her teeth.

Still, Jesse is the one hiding in the bushes while two of her best friends try to visit her. But their notion of intimacy seems to involve bonding with each other by trashing her, which doesn't exactly incline Jesse toward intimacy with either of them.

"I remember the first time I ever saw her," says Robert. "In the courtyard at Columbia. She looked almost other-worldly, with those cool blue eyes, like ice on the Himalayas. I guess I was challenged by her remoteness. I wanted to bring her back down to earth and roll her around in the mud."

Rachel laughs. "I know what you mean. I remember in our women's group she had this engaging country-girl innocence. When I told the group about sleeping with a woman, she looked like she'd never heard of such a thing. Naturally, it made me want to show her what it was all about. And I must say that she took to it like a horse to oats."

"I think she's afraid of getting too close to people," says Robert. "Her father killed himself. I always worried that it ran in the family, the way musical ability does."

Bingo, thinks Jesse, touched to discover that both understand her better than she has realized.

"He killed himself, yet Jesse always portrays him as this happy-go-lucky rascal," says Rachel.

"I never met the dude, but I've noticed that those bad-boy types are often closet alcoholics."

Hidden beneath a pile of crisp autumn leaves, head resting on her forearms, Jesse was an Apache warrior being chased by the cavalry. As she lay on the bottom of a pond, breathing through a hollow reed, soldiers in blue uniforms with crossed cartridge belts were ransacking the swamp all around her.

The dust from the dry leaves was sharp in her nostrils, making her want to sneeze, which she knew she mustn't do if she wanted to remain uncaptured. The leaves were tickling her forearms like dancing spiders. Using just her fingertips, she scratched.

Jesse heard her mother's familiar whistle from the back door—six notes from a song called "Deep Purple," which meant that supper was ready. She burst from the leaf pile, imagining that she was a blue gill leaping from a pond to snag a dragonfly. Dashing across the field, she combed dead leaves from her ponytail with her fingers. Over by his garage door Daryl was yelling, "Ollie, ollie, in free!" But she ignored him, bound for home.

Halfway to the house, Jesse froze behind a bush with thorns and mahogany-colored leaves. She was a fawn hiding from an approaching hunter, concealed by her spotted hide.

For a moment, the cicadas in the elm trees ceased their sawing, the grasshoppers paused in mid-jump, and the crickets swallowed their chirrups. The five hollow notes of a dove sounded from a nearby tree.

Jesse looked up quickly, but saw only juicy purple mulberries, hanging from the knotted branches like Jujyfruits you chewed at the movies. Her mother whistled again, her six notes blending with the dove's five.

Jesse pranced through the tall grass toward the back door, a Tennessee walking horse with weighted hooves, performing in the show of champions. She tossed her muzzle so her arched ponytail lashed.

Reaching the swings, she jumped on and pumped as hard as she could, chains screeching like jungle birds. Worried that she might swing right over the top and around the other side, as Daryl claimed he had once done, she stopped pumping and let the swing die. She was a paratrooper poised in the bay of a fighter-bomber, about to drop behind enemy lines. Letting go of the chains, she flew out of her seat, one hand pulling her parachute chord, the other cradling her machine gun. Hitting the ground, she rolled over and over to dodge enemy fire. Then she leapt to her feet and zigzagged to the house, spraying the Nazis with bullets as she ran.

As she hurtled through the back door, safe at last, her mother looked up from the stove. "You're late. Where were you?"

"Out back, playing with Daryl."

"What were you playing?" Her mother glanced down at her grass-stained feet.

Jesse hesitated. She had played so many things. How did you explain this to an adult who seemed to be only one thing all the time? "Magic Circle."

Her father appeared, tie loosened, collar unbuttoned, rolling his starched shirtsleeves to his elbows. "Hey, darling."

"Daddy! You're back!" She hurled herself at him. He swept her up to the ceiling, then settled her on his hip. "Where did you say you went?" she asked, patting his cute, fuzzy bald spot, a nest in the middle of his thick black hair.

"To a convention in Newport News."

"Where's that?"

"Over on the shore."

"What's a convention?"

"A bunch of morons get together and lie about all the deals they've cut." He glanced at her mother with a crooked smile, squinting in the smoke from the cigarette that dangled from the corner of his mouth.

"Why would they want to do that?"

"You got me, buddy. It's called business."

They sat down at the round wooden table in the corner of the kitchen. Her mother had put some yellow flowers in a glass vase in the middle of the table, and they were using the green cloth napkins. She always tried to make things special when Jesse's father got home from a trip.

"Mommy, I heard that mourning dove again. Just now, out in the yard."

"That's nice, dear."

"But why would it sing in the evening?"

Her mother glanced at her. "Why wouldn't it?"

"I thought it was supposed to sing in the morning."

Her mother frowned. Then she smiled. "Oh, I get it. It's not a morning dove, darling, it's a mourning dove. M-O-U-R-N-I-N-G." Remembering that Jesse couldn't spell yet, she said, "It's two different words. One means early in the day. The other means you're sad because someone has died or gone away."

"Why is the dove sad?"

"Maybe it isn't. Maybe it just sounds that way."

"Maybe it's lost its mate," said her father. "They say that if you shoot one, the other calls for it the rest of its life." Raising his dark, bushy eyebrows, he looked at her mother.

"Why would someone want to shoot one?" asked Jesse.

"People eat them. They're considered a delicacy."

"I don't think that's very nice."

"Kiddo, sometimes life ain't very nice."

"Isn't," murmured her mother.

"I think life is nice," Jesse said.

"Check in with me again when you're fifty," suggested her father.

After supper they sat on the back porch. Her mother lit a Camel, leaving a ring of scarlet lipstick around one end. Sucking on his reed, her father slipped together the pieces of his clarinet. Jesse stood beside him, watching this transformation of sections of wood into a long black tube that could make sounds like a baby crying for its mother, or water bubbling up from a spring, or a wild cat yowling in the forest. As her father tightened the screws that held the reed to the mouthpiece, Jesse heard the dove calling in the yard.

"Listen!" she ordered her parents.

Both paused, while a bat on insect patrol swooped past, silhouetted against the scarlet sky. The dove's five notes echoed from the woods. Holding the clarinet to his lips, her father mimicked the call. They waited, but the dove didn't reply.

Her father began to play, repeating the five notes in different rhythms and keys. Jesse watched her mother's unhappy look change into a soft smile as her father became more and more daring, like when Daryl showed off for Jesse, doing a handstand on his bicycle handlebars, or making his bicycle rear and twist in midair like a stallion.

The song faded into another Jesse had never heard before. Her mother exhaled a stream of smoke that curled to the rafters and drifted out the screen into the night sky. Then she started singing in her deep voice, "...Can't go on. Everything I had is gone. Stormy weather. Since my man and I ain't together...."

That summer Jesse and Daryl spent their free time sneaking from tree to tree out back, trying to track the dove calls. They rigged traps of string and sticks, baiting them with pieces of Baby Ruth. At Sunday school the deacon showed them a picture of the Holy Ghost, a white bird with outspread wings, flying straight down like an airplane in a nosedive. They decided a mourning dove must look like that. The eerie call from the woods between their houses at dawn and at dusk became a backdrop to their games and chores. But they never saw one.

Jesse realizes that now that she's fifty, she can't check in with her father as he recommended that night so long ago. As Robert pointed out, he's dead.

She hears a discreet meow. Looking down, she discovers her cat Sadie sitting in the poison ivy, jet black against the green, tail wrapped carefully around her front paws, staring up at Jesse through neon gold eyes. Jesse smiles faintly. Sadie narrows her eyes. Jesse blows her a silent kiss. Sadie starts to purr.

Thor lifts his head from his paws. His ears and nostrils quiver. He glances in every direction, long ears swaying. Spotting the cat, he cocks his head.

Before Thor can get up and bound over, something rustles in the undergrowth. Sadie is transformed from a family pet into a serial killer. She crouches. She listens. She creeps forward on flexing paws. Bursting from the bushes like a torpedo, she streaks across the grass to the far side of the pool and, with one leap, vanishes down the hillside, ignoring Robert, who is calling, "Sadie! What's up? Come say hello to the old man!"

Robert returns his attention to Rachel. Her voice is so low and his grin so lascivious that Jesse knows she's saying something dirty. He reaches out and pinches her nipple, stiff beneath her bathing suit.

Please God, pleads Jesse, don't let them make love. They begin to touch each other in ways she remembers each touching her. Rachel's fingertips stroke Robert's cheek. Robert brushes the hair off Rachel's forehead with the back of his hand. Jesse can almost feel their combined caresses on her own flesh. Rachel's whispered endearments she can't decipher remind her of a faraway time when life had seemed much simpler.

Jesse's stomach clenches just as it did that night they took her to dinner on the lake and first confessed that they had slept together. She remembers the urge to plant her fork between Robert's eyes and her steak knife in Rachel's throat. This definitely isn't how she had hoped to spend her fiftieth birthday.

Rachel, bless her heart, pushes Robert away.

"What's the matter?"

"Don't be crazy. We can't do this here. What if Jesse comes home?"

"We'll hear the car in the driveway."

"Maybe she's not in a car. Maybe she's gone for a birthday hike. Maybe she's standing on that hill across the valley right now."

"So what if she is? You can't see here from there. I'll make it fast."

Rachel puts her hand on his furry chest to block his advance. "Sweetheart, you know I don't like it fast. It makes me feel like a handy household appliance."

Jesse's blood pressure returns to normal. She congratulates Rachel. Why did Jesse ever let her go? If she had just continued their four-way fray, she and Rachel might have gotten rid of Robert and Peter. Or Robert and Peter might have gotten rid of Rachel and her. Or....

Rachel has dragged Robert to the pool edge. She shoves him in. "Cool yourself off, my love."

God, thinks Jesse, that is one cute, tough woman. Forgetting her earlier enthusiasm for celibacy, she wonders how late is too late to change her mind.

Meanwhile, from the valley into which Sadie has plunged comes the sound of National Guard helicopters. The weekend warriors are moving up the cornfield. Stalks are whipping and lashing beneath their swirling blades. Bursts of Uzi-esque flapping get louder and louder, like an approaching locomotive. Terrific. There's nothing like the peace and quiet of country living.

As the five copters pass above the swimming pool like giant farting June bugs, Robert, who is standing in the shallow end with the whirlwinds scrambling his gray hair, raises both middle fingers above his head and shouts, "Goddamn fucking fascist pigs!" Conveniently forgetting that, since he's a judge now, he's a pillar of the Establishment. But Jesse can still glimpse the slender, bearded boy in his red bandana headband, whom she first spotted on the steps of the administration building at Columbia, wielding a clawed

Chippendale chair leg like a nightstick against advancing security guards.

Jesse and Daryl were standing by the cornfield in the valley below their houses, looking in every direction to make sure no one was watching. They started down a row marked by crossed sticks stuck in the soil. The sun lit their path with wavery yellow ribbons, while the pointed leaves clashed overhead like green swords. They came to a narrow break in the stalks to the right. Turning, they crossed several rows, then headed left up another row, following a route through the maze indicated by sticks and rocks. Eventually they arrived at a small clearing in the center of the field.

Removing their knapsacks, they took out two blue chenille bedspreads salvaged from Jesse's attic. She spread one across the dirt. Daryl suspended the other on stalks around the perimeter, to form a billowing ceiling. They were a pioneer couple in the wilderness who supplied all their needs by their own hands.

Jesse placed their wrapped tuna sandwiches and Cokes in the shade and made a neat stack of the fabric scraps from Daryl's mother's sewing room. Daryl disappeared among the stalks. When he returned, he was carrying three plump ears of corn, one with blond tassels, one with red, and the third with dark brown. Jesse, inspecting them, approved.

Sitting cross-legged, Daryl stripped back and trimmed the shucks to expose some kernels, which Jesse colored with Magic Markers to form blue or brown eyes, black nostrils, and red mouths. Using his Swiss army knife, Daryl drilled holes through the shucks into the ears and inserted Popsicle stick arms. With bits of ribbon, Jesse tied up their silky hair. Then both worked with scissors, needles, and thread to cut the scraps of fabric and sew them into outfits for their daughters.

When they finished, the sun was at an angle overhead. Sitting on the bedspread, they ate their sandwiches and drank Cokes. Then they stretched out for a nap, their new daughters arrayed between them.

"Aren't they beautiful?" murmured Jesse.

"How could they not be with you as their mother?" replied Daryl, touching her hair.

She smiled. His dark hair was hanging in his eyes. The boys at school made fun of his curls. But the girls sent him notes during class and blushed when he spoke to them.

"Do you know how real babies are made?" he asked, hands behind his head as he gazed up at the billowing blue ceiling, luminous from the summer sun.

"Of course," she said. "Everyone knows that."

"Do you want to try it?"

"I think we're too young."

"We could at least try."

"If it worked, we'd be in big trouble. My parents would never let me marry you. I'm only eleven years old."

"We could just pretend to make one," suggested Daryl. "You're already my wife, aren't you?"

"Yes. But what do you mean—pretend to make one?"

"You do it, but since you don't really want a baby, you don't get one."

"Are you sure that's how it works?"

"Yes, I think so."

"Okay. We can try it."

They did try it there in their pioneer cabin among the cornstalks with their adorable corncob daughters watching. Although they had no idea what they were doing, they liked it. Resting on the chenille bedspread afterwards, they heard a mourning dove calling nearby. Daryl jumped up and chased its receding call down the narrow rows, but he didn't manage to see it.

Jesse hears another car coming up the driveway, gravel crunching beneath its tires. Her birthday afternoon is beginning to resemble a model home tour.

The door slams. Thor leaps to his feet and careens past Jesse, barking like a German shepherd in a Nazi film. Robert claims they named him Thor, after the Norse god of thunder, because of this bark. But as Jesse recalls, it was a nickname for Thorazine, which she was considering taking at the time, their quadrangle having reached its pinnacle of complexity.

"Thor!" exclaims Cybele. "How you doing, old boy?"

Thor moans and whimpers. You would think from his desperation that Jesse has been doing cruel medical experiments on him in Cybele's absence. Thor slept on Cybele's bed for his first several years. Then Cybele left for college and he was exiled to a cushion in the entryway. Jesse is sure he's never forgiven her. No doubt he'll invent a way to expose her in her current predicament.

Thor and Cybele saunter past Jesse, Thor looking back and forth between the two women.

"Hey, Dad. Hey, Rachel," calls Cybele.

They climb out of the pool, Rachel giving Robert an I-told-you-so look. Cybele kisses both, avoiding their dripping bodies.

"So where's my short mother?" asks Cybele. The three laugh. Cybele calls Rachel her tall mother and Jesse her short mother.

"No idea," replies Robert. "Her towel and her robe are here, but she seems to have vanished."

"Do you think she's okay?"

Robert picks up on her impulse of panic. "Let's hope so," he says anxiously. "Relax, you two," says Rachel. "She's probably at the mall buying a new outfit for her party."

As Cybele strips down to her bikini, Jesse inspects the panther etched on her shoulder. Like a Neanderthal cave painter, the tattoo artist has used the jut of Cybele's shoulder blade to emphasize the panther's haunch. As Cybele turns to sit down, the sun glints off the gold hoop in her navel. She's searched high and low for eccentricities with which to outrage her parents. Unfortunately, ex-hippies have seen everything and done most of it. The only thing that really concerns Robert and herself is Cybele's devotion to her job as a stock analyst for Merrill Lynch.

Today Cybele is wearing a studded black leather armband around her bicep, no doubt a statement to her parents that they are pathetic aging practitioners of vanilla sex. Glancing down at her own body, Jesse recalls some of the feats her flesh has performed. Whatever Cybele may prefer to believe, this body has been around the block a few times more than Jesse cares to remember. The creative combinations of appendages and orifices—how have her joints survived the strain?

"Look, honey," says Robert, gesturing to the rings in Cybele's navel and his own earlobe. "We match."

"As if," replies Cybele with a grimace that Jesse interprets as meaning, "Dream on, you old goat. You wish your pitiful little hippie hoop was as cool as my really awesome navel piercing."

"So," says Robert, "how's the market this week?"

"Yeah, right," says Cybele. "Like, you really care."

"But I do. I'm starting to think a lot about how to maintain my standard of living when I retire."

"Retire? But, Dad, you've just been appointed judge."

"I know, but I have a lot more years behind me now than I do ahead of me."

"It's Jesse who's supposed to be thinking like that today," says Rachel.

"I guess having someone I met when she was twenty-one turn fifty is sobering for me as well."

"Get over it," suggests Cybele with the insensitivity of the young to the issues of their elders.

"I was trying to," snaps Robert. "By asking you about the market."

They sit in strained silence.

"I was wondering if you'd take a look at my pension plan and tell me what you think of my investments," says Robert, trying hard.

"Not a problem," says Cybele, accepting his olive branch. "Have your assistant fax me a list of your holdings on Monday, and I'll be happy to tell you what I think."

"I'd really appreciate it."

Jesse is astonished. There are three possibilities, each equally alarming: Robert is trying to bond with Cybele via the stock market. Robert is putting Cybele on and will laugh about it later with Rachel. Or Robert is having a midlife crisis. How can he scream at the National Guard one minute, then ask his daughter's advice about Wall Street the next? With relief she realizes that Robert's mental health is now Rachel's problem, not hers.

"I have something to tell you guys," announces Cybele. "I can't wait any longer, so I guess I'll have to tell Mom separately."

Jesse feels the hairs stand up along the back of her neck. Is she pregnant? HIV positive?

"What?" asks Robert, equally alarmed by the solemnity of her tone. Jesse has always adored the seriousness with which he takes his role as Cybele's father, despite everything.

"I know you aren't going to like it, but Karl and I are getting married this fall. By an Episcopal priest."

Robert's mouth drops open. He glances at Rachel.

Good for you, thinks Jesse. You've finally found a way to shock your parents—by marrying your childhood sweetheart. Karl's father, Aaron, will freak out when he hears the priest bit.

"Why?" asks Rachel.

"Because we love each other."

"Fine, but why wreck it by getting married?" asks Robert.

"We're not like you guys. We want to make a commitment before God to live together all our lives in peace and fidelity."

Rachel and Robert look at each other.

"You both got married," says Cybele. "Why shouldn't we?"

"Yes," says Rachel, "but we didn't stay married."

"And we certainly weren't peaceful or faithful," adds Robert.

Jesse smiles as she stands there in the poison ivy, tickled by this endless interplay between the generations, each believing itself to be correcting the failings of the previous one.

"I want Karl to be my husband for the rest of our lives."

"Uh, how do you know?" asks Robert, trying to sound respectful.

"Know that I want to be with Karl for the rest of my life?" asks Cybele irritably.

"You're just out of business school. How could you possibly know now what you want for the rest of your life?"

"Dad," says Cybele, rolling her eyes. "Like, you just know, okay?"

"You think you know," mutters Robert.

"Whatever," says Cybele.

Jesse was packed up and sent to boarding school at the National Cathedral in Washington, D.C., ostensibly so that she could sing with the Cathedral choir. Her mother informed her that she wasn't going to waste her voice, as her mother had hers. Daryl and she yearned and suffered. Every vacation they were inseparable, vowing to marry as soon as they could. His mother, a widow, couldn't afford to send him to college, so he planned to train in the army for a career.

During Jesse's senior year, her mother divorced her father and married a man who owned a gas station in the next town. When Jesse went home the summer before Julliard, her father sat on the back porch after work every evening, smoking Camels, drinking Jack Daniels, and playing plaintive tunes on his clarinet, as though trying to pipe his wife home.

It didn't work. One evening during Jesse's Christmas vacation, he hanged himself from the mulberry tree out back. Jesse found him the next day. His body swayed stiffly in the winter gusts and his ravaged face was blue.

The following year Jesse's mother was diagnosed with ovarian cancer and died within six months. When Jesse went home for the funeral, she stayed with Daryl's mother. Daryl was flying a helicopter in Vietnam. The afternoon after her mother's service, she and Mrs. Morris sat in the den drinking tea.

"Remember when you and Daryl were kids?" said Mrs. Morris. "Each day was like a safari. You'd get so excited over the least little thing. Like that bird you chased around the woods all the time."

"Mourning doves. We never did manage to see one."

"I always felt so bad for you, Jesse," said Mrs. Morris, "with your parents running around on each other like that."

Jesse looked at her. "What do you mean?"

Recognizing her slip too late, Mrs. Morris jumped up, grabbed the teapot, and headed for the kitchen.

Jesse pointed at Mrs. Morris's chair. "I don't care for any more tea, thank you, Mrs. Morris. I just want to know what you meant by that."

"Oh, honey, I shouldn't have gone telling tales out of school."

"Please. I need to know."

Mrs. Morris said Jesse's mother had been seeing the gas station owner for several years before her divorce, and there had been another man before him. But Jesse's father's "conventions" weren't always for business. For the first time, Jesse figured out that her birthday was only six months after her parents' marriage.

Back at Julliard, Jesse buried herself in work. One night in her carrel at the library, as she read troubadour lyrics for her Early Music course, she came across a chanson by Bernart of Ventadour that ended, "She has taken my heart. / She has taken my self. / She has taken from me the world. / And then she has eluded me, / Leaving me with only my desire / And my parched heart."

This was what had happened to her father, Jesse realized as she traced with her index finger some graffiti etched into her desktop. Apparently it was the nature of love to bring you great joy, followed by greater suffering. She wanted nothing more to do with it, except as a topic through which to earn her degree.

She wrote her thesis on Bernart of Ventadour, spending a year at the University of Toulouse. She made pilgrimages around the Languedoc to the towns and ruined castles associated with the various troubadours. She took classes in Old Provencal so she could read chansons in the original. She underwent training in the currently accepted modes for singing the lyrics. The best of the troubadours used physical love as a metaphor for spiritual love. If you followed their recipe, you could bypass the earthly variety altogether.

During her year in France, Jesse's replies to Daryl's letters from Vietnam became increasingly sporadic. Eventually, they stopped altogether. She had no intention of repeating her parents' mistakes. The mulberry tree was not her destination of choice.

Back in New York, applying for a teaching job at Columbia, she met Robert, a Maoist law student with a full beard and a bandana headband. He believed that love, like religion, was an opiate for the masses. Having in common a horror of love, he and Jesse "had sex." They were comrades, roommates, friends, anything but lovers.

One evening after Jesse moved into Robert's apartment on Riverside Drive in Harlem, she was lying on their bed scanning a newly discovered score for one of her favorite chansons, softly singing the notes. Robert was in the living room watching mayhem from Vietnam on the tube. Right outside the window she heard a mourning dove. The lonely call echoed down the red brick canyon formed by the walls of opposing apartment buildings.

Startled, Jesse padded into the living room.

"What's up?" asked Robert, glancing up from the television. "You look like you've seen a ghost."

"I just heard a mourning dove," Jesse replied. "I never knew they lived in cities. I used to hear them all the time back home in Virginia. But I never managed to see one."

"Jesus," he said. "They're all over the place. Look." He pulled up the blind and there on the fire escape perched a plump brown bird with a breast mottled as though with food stains.

"You mean, that's it?" Just then the bird's doughy chest quivered and it emitted its unearthly call.

"Cousins to pigeons. Rats with wings," Robert announced.

"I prefer how I pictured them in my head."

"That's your whole problem, Jesse. You live too much in your head." Each new atrocity on the evening news energized him, whereas all Jesse wanted was to lock herself up with her troubadours, who passed their days longing for some disembodied beloved.

One day Robert decided that he and Jesse needed to stop head tripping and develop subsistence skills like workers the world over. So they joined the stream of exhausted war protesters from Boston, New York, and Philadelphia who were moving to Vermont to recreate America's pre-industrial past by baling each other's hay, caponizing each other's roosters, and eating the placentas at each other's home births.

To bring in some cash, Jesse taught music appreciation at a local college, and Robert worked for Legal Aid. Eventually Cybele arrived, squalling and irresistible. Jesse soon realized that she was now firmly rooted in the life and loves of the flesh.

This idyll lasted twelve years.

One spring morning Robert woke up, turned to Jesse, and announced, "If the good Lord had meant us to have gardens, He wouldn't have given us supermarkets."

"She," murmured Jesse, who had recently joined a consciousness-raising group with nine other women, who spent most of their time complaining about having to can and freeze while their men plotted the revolution over bottles of bad wine. One member, a lanky therapist from North Carolina named Rachel, had recently confessed that she was having an affair with a woman. The women's group went into a state of collective shock. This was indeed an alternative to canning and freezing.

"Hey, Dad, what's this?" asks Cybele, pointing at the gold foil package lying in the shade beside Thor.

Jesse can hear the clanking of a tractor spreading manure in the pasture across the road. Thor's nostrils are twitching. Presumably, he can already smell it. Swarms of seagulls have arrived from the lake and are squawking over worms and insects.

"A present for your mother," says Robert.

"Cool. What is it?"

"A tee shirt."

"A tee shirt?" says Cybele. "For her fiftieth birthday? That's pretty lame, Dad."

"One present among several," he assures her. "Besides, what it says is really neat."

"Neat?" repeats Cybele with a mocking grin.

"Awesome?" asks Robert.

Robert has always claimed to be the first to use the term "groovy." Jesse muses that it must be humiliating for him now to be, like, so deeply uncool.

"What does it say?" asks Cybele.

"You'll just have to wait and see."

Jesse watches the gray-green leaves of the Russian olives shimmy in a breeze that is tickling her shoulders. She finally picks up the acrid odor of the manure. Then she realizes that the breeze at her back is actually a mosquito, which has just bitten her. She can hear it, plump with her own blood, buzzing like a cargo plane around her left ear. She spots another on her right forearm. An entire squadron must have received word that fresh meat is standing helpless in the Russian olives. If she slaps, she'll give herself away. So she grits her teeth and endures the bites. Surely her guests will leave soon? Shouldn't everyone be changing for the party?

She studies the three of them, cross-legged in a circle on her watermelon beach towel, Thor lying with his head in Cybele's lap. Cybele is kneading his favorite spot, just behind his ears.

Sadie stalks out of the weeds beyond the pool, eying this domestic scene disdainfully. Even as she walks, she is in transition from the Beast back into Beauty. She rubs the length of her silky black body along Rachel's thigh. Rachel narrows her green eyes, catlike, the way she always does when experiencing a gratuitous frisson.

Jesse studies the tableau. Of all living creatures, these are the ones most important to her. All of a sudden, on the afternoon of her fiftieth birthday, with the dog-day sun low in the sky, Jesse realizes that she is a fortunate woman. During her five decades, despite her attempts to evade it, she has given and received more than her share of love. On the balance sheet of her days to date, pleasure exceeds pain. Nearly insane from the need to scratch, she feels gratitude well up inside her. She lowers her head in thanks.

"Time to get ready for Jesse's picnic," announces Robert, getting to his feet. Rachel and Cybele follow him from the pool, past Jesse, down to the driveway. Thor noses Cybele's hanging hand. Sadie brings up the rear with a bearing that suggests she has planned to go to the driveway all along, and is not merely trailing along behind these sorry humans and their ridiculous dog.

The cars roll down the driveway. Clawing her bites, Jesse emerges from the Russian olives and notices her present lying forgotten by the pool house. Walking over, she picks it up. She slips off the maroon ribbon and opens the taped flaps. Pulling out a large gold tee shirt, she shakes it open and holds it up. It reads, "NIFTY AT FIFTY."

Half a dozen bats swirl down from the pool house loft where they have been napping all afternoon, upside down along the beams like miniature umbrellas. Bullfrogs by the cattle pond start to croak, viola da gamba tuning up for a twilight sonata. The distant lake gleams like a pool of molten lava. A mourning dove coos from the cornfield.

Jesse slips the tee shirt over her head and arranges it around her chest. She heads for the house to wash the poison ivy juice off her toes, put on some slacks, and grab her car keys.

It is time to boogie by the lakeshore in the glow from the setting sun.

GOD'S COUNTRY

Paulo slid back the grated door so Sidney could enter the elevator cage. Sidney nodded to Jesse, who was sitting on the carpeted banquette. She smiled back.

"On your way to rehearsal?" Jesse pointed at his black clarinet case. So far, Sidney had proved the friendliest person in her apartment building, so she was playing him for all he was worth. Otherwise, she would pass entire weekends in New York speaking to no one, apart from discussing the weather with the elevator men, just as she had done in Vermont with the postmistress and the checkout clerks at the IGA.

"Yes."

Behind his thick lenses, Sidney's gray eyes had a distracted look. Jesse wondered if he were running through the score for that night's opera in his head. Although she gathered he was about her age, he had an unwrinkled, choirboy face.

"What's the opera?" asked Jesse.

"*The Trojans.*"

"Do you like it?"

"It's interesting. Long, though. Five hours. But you should definitely see it. Maybe I can get you a ticket for tonight."

"That would be wonderful."

"I'll look into it, then."

As they exited the building, Sidney said, "Have a nice day."

"Thanks." Jesse turned to contemplate the doorway, encircled with Neo-Gothic stone oak leaves and acorns. She had picked her apartment because it was three blocks from Lincoln Center. Her daughter Cybele had a good job in Burlington as a stockbroker and had recently married her childhood sweetheart, Karl. Her ex-husband, Robert, was also living happily in Burlington with her best friend and former lover, Rachel. Jesse had suddenly realized that she was a free woman. She had wasted her voice when she was young, despite her mother's warnings, and now it was too late to sing professionally. It wasn't too late, though, for her to enjoy what smarter singers were doing with *their* voices.

But she felt like a fraud as she struggled toward the Food Emporium, hunched over against the wind whipping down Broadway. Overhead signs were rattling, and newspaper pages were swirling from trash baskets across the windshields of careening taxis. She had spent her childhood in a small town in Virginia and her adulthood outside of an even smaller town in Vermont. Apart from her years at the National Cathedral School in Washington and at Julliard in New York, she was a country girl. What made her think she could cope alone in the world's most relentless city? Her Vermont friends wouldn't even visit her, regarding New York as one huge, filthy, maximum-security prison. Her temp agency had assigned her to a bond trader named Kostas Powers, and sometimes the subway ride to his office overlooking Battery Park felt as alarming as Dante's trip through the Inferno.

Passing the entrance to the Sony IMAX movie theater, Jesse heard a man calling, "Help me. Won't somebody please help a blind man?" Looking around, she spotted an old man in a tattered overcoat sitting on the sidewalk surrounded by bulging plastic bags, a white cane across his lap. Although he repeated his request over and over like a stuck record, everyone walked past without looking at him.

Jesse stood there studying him. During her months in New York, she had tried to understand the callousness. There was so much misery in the streets that you tuned it out for self-protection. But she hadn't yet mastered this skill. She was accustomed to tuning *into* her environment—the call of a bird, the faint scarlet hint of fall at the tops of trees—if only to escape total sensory deprivation in the more placid countryside.

Walking over, Jesse looked down at the man. "Do you need some help?"

He lifted his shaggy, Lear-like head. His eye sockets looked blasted, and his irises were cloudy. What must it feel like, Jesse wondered, to be sightless and alone in the streets of New York, unable to summon any assistance? She was flooded with shame for her species.

"Of course I need help," he snarled. "Why else do you think I'm asking for it?"

Jesse blinked. "Well, here I am. What can I do for you, sir?"

"I need a taxi uptown to the New York Home for the Blind."

"Wait here," said Jesse. "I'll get one."

Standing on the curb, she hailed an empty cab. As she opened the back door, she said to the driver, a Singh in a soiled turban, "It's not for me. It's for him." She gestured to the man in his ragged overcoat, sprawled against the brick wall of the theater.

"Forget it," said the driver.

"But he needs a ride to the Home for the Blind."

"Please close my door."

Jesse did, and the taxi roared off.

Twice more she flagged down taxis and twice more their responses were similar.

Returning to the blind man, she said, "I'm sorry, but no one will take you."

"Keep trying. This happens all the time. Eventually someone will have a heart."

Returning to the curb, Jesse hailed two more taxis with the same results. She was alarmed to realize how drastically city living dehumanized people. In Vermont, flotillas of cars, trucks, ATVs, snowmobiles, bicycles, and dog sleds would have vied with each other to escort the old man home.

"I'm sorry," she told him, "but this is impossible."

"I should have known no one would help me. And you're just like all the rest!"

"But I've been *trying* to help you."

"But you didn't succeed, did you? Your noble intentions do me no good whatsoever."

"Look here," she snapped, forgetting that he couldn't look anywhere, "I just wasted fifteen minutes on you, and all you can do is criticize me. It's not my fault. This is your horrible city, not mine!"

"Don't exaggerate. You wasted five minutes, maximum."

Why am I taking this? Jesse asked herself. "Well, good luck!" She marched off, swearing she had just performed her last act of mercy.

"Wait, lady! Please don't go. Don't leave me here alone."

Jesse stopped, while pedestrians too smart to have gotten involved streamed past her. In Virginia or Vermont she would have been considered responsible for solving this man's predicament, but in New York City she was the only one dumb enough not to know better.

She returned to the old man. "All right, I'll stay. But I have to tell you that your attitude is appalling. If you want help, you need to act pleasant and grateful. Whatever you may really feel."

He appeared to think this over. "Okay. I'm sorry I was rude. I'm just so tired and frustrated."

"Well, so is everyone else. So stop feeling sorry for yourself."

He shook his shaggy head in amused disbelief.

"And another thing," said Jesse. "No wonder no one will help you. You look like a drunk."

"What am I supposed to do about that? I can't see how I look."

"You could at least comb your hair and wear some clean clothes. Now, get up and come to the curb with me. When someone stops, I'll help you in. Then I'll shut the door and walk away. You can browbeat the poor driver on your own."

He struggled to rise without success. Jesse grabbed his arm and hoisted him to his feet. Then she gathered his cane and plastic bags. Holding her arm, he hobbled to the curb.

Realizing what this was all about, she said, "You need money for the cab."

"No, I have money. I don't need money. I need a cab."

Seeing one approach with the appropriate roof light lit, Jesse waved it towards her. It swerved out of the traffic and pulled up alongside the curb. The driver, a young man in a backward baseball cap with a gold hoop through one earlobe, took a good long look at the blind man and roared away, barely escaping a collision with a passing van.

Jesse began to suspect that she might have to hand-deliver this man to his home. Or maybe she could wave a ten-dollar bill at the driver to lure him into stopping. It would be worth at least ten dollars to get rid of this wretched old man.

Another empty cab appeared. Jesse jumped up and down to get the driver's attention. The taxi stopped before them. Jesse wrenched open the door, expecting the driver, a black man with a gleaming bald head, to take off with his back door flapping when he spotted his new passenger. She shoved the blind man into the rear seat and tossed his cane and plastic bags in after him. The driver's mouth opened to protest. Jesse slammed the door and raced across the sidewalk, through the revolving door, and into the crowded lobby of the movie theater.

Deeply relieved to have passed the buck of human decency to some other sucker, she watched through the window as the old man yelled at the driver. The driver's face assumed a long-suffering expression. The taxi pulled away from the curb and nosed into the stream of uptown traffic.

Later, waiting for the elevator in her lobby stood a ruddy-faced middle-aged man Jesse had passed several times in the street. The whites of his eyes were bloodshot. Noticing her struggle with her plastic Food Emporium bags, he asked, "Can I help you?"

"Thanks, but I'm fine." She lined up her four bags on the mosaic floor.

"I'm your downstairs neighbor, Steve Ryan. But everyone calls me Ryan."

She held out her hand. "Jesse Stern." Remembering that she was taking back her maiden name, she said, "Jesse Phillips, I mean."

"I hear you're from Vermont?"

"Yes."

"It's hard to believe someone would want to leave God's country to move to New York City."

"You know Vermont?"

"I went to summer camp there when I was a boy. A Quaker work camp in the Green Mountains. My kids went there too."

"Vermont is beautiful. But I lived there for thirty years. I realized there might be more to life than beauty."

"Well, you're in the right place, then: you won't find any beauty here."

"I guess that depends on how you define beauty."

"As for me, I'm trying to figure out how to get *out* of New York. But it's not easy if your career is advertising."

Nodding to Paulo, Jesse walked into the elevator with Ryan behind her. As the cage rose, she glanced at Ryan's square jaw. Then at his left hand, which bore no wedding band. He had mentioned children, but of course she had a child too.

Jesse realized this was the first time she had felt so much as a twinge of desire since Robert and Rachel pulled their double betrayal by falling in love with each other while both were supposedly in love with her. She was alarmed to discover that the boa constrictor of lust that used to threaten to squeeze the life out of her wasn't entirely dead yet. But why a man?

They arrived at Ryan's floor and he got off.

"So, Paulo," said Jesse as they resumed their ascent, "how are you today?"

He smiled. "Not so bad. But tired."

She studied his olive face and curly black hair. He had bruised circles under his eyes. "Late night last night?"

Paulo nodded. "But worth it."

"Oh?" said Jesse cautiously, not eager to hear about his love life.

"Yes, I won the Latin Showcase competition at Roseland."

"You're kidding!" Jesse studied him in his navy blue uniform with the gold trim up the legs and around the cuffs and collar. "Congratulations. Which dance is your specialty?"

"The cha cha."

"How do you know the cha cha?"

"I was a doorman at the Copa. I watched the dancers and picked it up."

They reached her floor.

"Well, I'm impressed," said Jesse.

Paulo smiled and gave a little bow.

Lying on her doormat was a white envelope. Inside were two opera tickets and a note from Sidney wishing her an enjoyable evening.

Studying the tickets, Jesse tried to decide whom to invite to the opera. She dialed a friend from Julliard days, but got her answering machine. Then she tried a family friend from

Virginia who was staying at the Plaza, but she was out. She wondered about Ryan. Surely, after her experience with Robert and Rachel, she had learned not to go looking for love anymore. Human beings were the only creatures dumb enough to stake their entire emotional well-being on relationships that common sense should tell them would eventually end, one way or another. Still, while they lasted, they were so delicious. And she was lonely. Looking up Ryan's number, she called him.

"Ryan here." He sounded angry.

"Hello, this is Jesse Phillips."

"Yes?" He didn't appear to recognize her name.

"We met in the elevator just now. I'm your upstairs neighbor."

"Yes?" His tone of voice didn't change. Damn. He wasn't pleased to hear from her. Why waste a good ticket?

"I was worried that I sometimes play my stereo too loudly."

"I never hear a thing."

"Well, if it ever bothers you, don't hesitate to tell me."

"Oh, I won't," he said with a curt laugh. "New Yorkers never hesitate to complain."

"Okay. Just checking." She felt as awkward as a teenager.

"Well, see you around, Jesse. Thanks for calling." He sounded a bit warmer. At least he remembered her name.

"Talk to you later, Ryan. Bye."

She slammed down the phone. How could she have been so stupid? She had just met him, for God's sake. After all these years of marriage, motherhood, and rural adultery, she had forgotten about the need to play hard to get.

Walking across the paved courtyard toward the huge glass and steel opera house, which glittered with lights like a jewel in the night, Jesse spotted several people standing outside the entrances waving tickets for sale. She decided to do the same with her extra one so it wouldn't go to waste. She would give the proceeds to Sidney. She stationed herself by the revolving door and held up the ticket. Apparently, it wasn't a popular opera; people weren't wandering around searching for tickets as they usually did.

Finally a man with a mane of silver hair came up. His navy blue cashmere overcoat was worn but well tailored, and he wore a Black Watch plaid scarf around his neck. "Excuse me. That ticket—I can see by the way it's punched that it's complimentary. If the guards catch you selling it, you'll get in trouble."

Jesse held it up in the light from inside. He pointed out the telltale holes.

"Thanks for telling me. I didn't realize I wasn't supposed to sell it. Somebody gave it to me."

"I'd hate to see you have a problem when you don't know any better."

"I really appreciate that. Would you like it? Otherwise, it will go to waste."

He hesitated. "Sure. Thanks."

Jesse handed it to him. "I hope you enjoy the opera."

"Oh, I will. I've already seen it three times this season."

"That's quite a recommendation."

"Yes, I'm sure you'll like it."

Jesse walked through the revolving door. Passing the ticket takers, she descended the carpeted stairway to orchestra level. As she stood to one side of the bar, she watched all the trampoline-faced New York women drift past, some draped in furs. No one returned her gaze. Her undyed hair was streaked with gray. Her quilted down overcoat belonged on the steppes. Her lip liner followed the actual contours of her lips.

As Jesse searched for her seat, she reflected that she was worse than a fraud—she was an *obvious* fraud. Any true New

Yorker could have picked her out right away as a hick. As she sat down, she decided it didn't matter. There was no law against a hick's attending cultural events.

The man she had given the ticket to slid into the next seat. She hadn't realized that he would of course be sitting beside her. She smiled and nodded. He nodded back and settled in.

Jesse supposed he was one of the aficionados she had read about, who attended the opera several times a week, who knew the scores by heart, who realized when a singer missed a note, who knew which performances merited a bravo or brava.

The conductor came out and the crowd applauded. Jesse searched for Sidney in the orchestra pit but couldn't find him. The overture began. The man slid lower in his seat and wrapped his cashmere overcoat around himself.

The curtain rose, and Cassandra proclaimed dire prophecies for Troy from the city walls. The man closed his eyes and laid his silver head against the seat back.

Soldiers fought and women wailed. The shadow of the huge wooden horse loomed against the backdrop. The man beside Jesse snored softly. As the room heated up, he began to smell like spoiled cat food.

By intermission, Jesse had figured out that this man was very clever. Having nowhere else to go, he was taking the opportunity to get several hours of sleep in a warm and comfortable seat, surrounded by people intent on watching the stage rather than on robbing him. But his stench had become unbearable.

She left the opera house, strolling home down dimly lit side streets, trying to imagine what series of events had landed that man on the streets. Without the money from her parents' estate, the same thing could easily happen to her. Though Robert would probably rescue her, from guilt if not from love. Cybele would certainly rescue her.

When Jesse rang for the elevator the next morning, Basil was on duty. The previous month when her computer broke down, he had repaired it for free in about thirty seconds. It seemed that when he wasn't operating an elevator, he was a computer genius.

As they descended, Basil asked, "Did you hear about Sidney?"

"Hear what about Sidney?"

"Dropped dead of a heart attack walking home from the opera last night."

"Sidney?"

"Horrible, huh?"

"I can't believe it. I was talking to him right here in this very spot yesterday. He seemed fine. He gave me tickets to the opera."

"Yeah, I guess you never know when your number's up."

Jesse headed down the sidewalk toward the subway. It didn't seem fair. Sidney was so young, so pleasant. She was just getting to know him. They might have become friends.

As she rounded the corner, Steve Ryan, dressed in a pinstriped suit and swigging from a Starbuck's cup, almost ran her down.

"So how's it going?" asked Ryan.

"Not so great. I just heard about Sidney's heart attack."

"Heart attack?"

"Didn't you hear? Apparently he dropped dead in the street last night."

Ryan grimaced. "You think Sidney died of a heart attack?"

"That's what Basil told me in the elevator just now."

"Sidney was murdered."

"What?"

Ryan shook his head. "Sidney ran a drug ring from his apartment. He also had a stable of prostitutes. Several women he had gotten hooked on heroin banded together and killed him. Good riddance to bad rubbish, I say."

Jesse stared at Ryan. "But he seemed so sweet."

Ryan shrugged. "I think you must have been hiding out in God's country for too long, Jesse. In New York things are rarely what they seem."

THE POLITICS OF PARADISE

As the ferry pulled into the sagging wooden dock, Ryan knew he was about to disembark on Eden. The deserted Conch Cay beaches, pink from ground-up shells, were the most spectacular in the Caribbean, worthy of a back cover on *The New Yorker*. Seagulls swept down, mewing and fighting over scraps discarded by two men cleaning bonefish on the pier. Half-wild tiger cats darted in and out, dodging the flying knives, vying with the gulls for their share. Ryan grabbed his suitcases and clambered onto the dock.

The village was as he remembered it: several dozen pink, light green, or bare weathered wood houses in various stages of collapse, huddled around the cove, seeking shelter from the hurricanes that pounded the ocean side of the island. Beached motorboats. Sidewalks of packed sand. Rustling palm trees that dwarfed all these puny works of man. The drone and clatter of electric generators. The Primitive Baptist church with its eternally burning light bulb over the doorway—a fitting tribute to Christ on this island where electricity was almost as precious as fresh water. And over everything, the vast blue sky and searing sun.

Eight hours ago in New York City, icy winds had howled down narrow streets. Snow swirled around the tall project buildings in Spanish Harlem as Ryan's taxi carried him to LaGuardia. A jet to Miami, a DC-7 to Orono Island, a ferry twelve miles across Orono Bay to Conch Cay. Like a snake shedding a tattered skin, he had fled the collapsing civilization that had spawned him. No longer would he go in a pinstriped suit to an Art Deco office building on Madison Avenue to write copy for new and improved Stir 'n Serve Pudding. No longer would he jockey for recognition from R. L. Marsh, senior copy chief. No longer would he pick up the phone at his apartment on the Upper West Side to hear Elaine in Connecticut itemizing the ways he had failed her and the children. Instead of looking out his office window to a flashing sign to learn the temperature, he needed only to look at the sky now and feel the sun on his bare forearms. Rather than trying to convince housewives to buy a carcinogenic mix of chemicals, he would supply people with fresh food and comfortable shelter at his newly purchased inn. His entire life would take on an uncharacteristic integrity.

Ryan had made one unbreakable rule: he must keep to himself on Conch Cay. Human interaction in the past had led to nothing but disillusion and disappointment. Once he had been young and in love—with a Cornell coed in a cashmere sweater set and pearls, a Tri Delt he met while making Kleenex carnations for the Easter Seals float in the Spring Fling parade. Their marriage had accomplished little but saddling Ryan with responsibilities, the fulfillment of which had robbed him of his credibility by requiring him to do and say things he didn't really believe. Just as he had pared down his belongings to the contents of these two suitcases, so had he pared down his involvement with other people. Elaine would get her money every month, but he wouldn't have to listen to her litany of complaints every night. And he would not become entangled again. He felt like a pioneer on the Oregon Trail, casting aside household possessions for passage over the Rockies.

During the divorce he couldn't sleep, couldn't eat. His wife of twenty-six years loved some balding investment banker. Jessica and Kevin were grown, off to Vassar and Yale. Ryan himself was graying, impotent, bypassed for promotion to copy chief. Burnt out. Self-respect was gone, but so were the wife and children for whom he had sacrificed it. He descended into a pit of self-loathing. But then one day he impulsively cashed in his Keogh to buy the Conch Cay Inn from Ed Norton.

And here he was, reborn, a new and improved life ahead of him.

Ryan strode up the sand sidewalk past a gaggle of small children, blond and sunburned, grinning shyly and whispering to one another. His inn was soon before him—two buildings, one a long low line of bedrooms, the other a bar and dining room. Listing palms swayed over both.

Three years ago he, Elaine, and the Achesons, after a day of nude sunbathing at the far end of the island, had anchored their rented sailboat in Conch Cay harbor and rowed the dinghy ashore for dinner at this inn—native lobster, conch chowder, turtle steak, fresh vegetables, papayas, coconut pie. They sat drinking gin under the palms until dawn, talking loudly, laughing, and pretending that Elaine didn't wish Ryan were some balding banker named Stan.

Ryan stood behind the massive wooden bar polishing glasses and watching Ida set the dining tables on the screened porch. He had read in a history book left behind by Ed Norton that Ida's four-times-great-grandparents had owned vast stretches of South Carolina. They had fled to Conch Cay with their herds and slaves during the American Revolution. The thin topsoil soon became depleted, and crops began to fail. The slaves moved to their own cay. Ida's forebears began a numb struggle for subsistence. They fished. They hunted wild boar, descendants of pigs left to propagate as a meat supply by passing pirates. They went to sea in homemade boats to dive for sponges. They walked mules with lanterns around their necks up and down the dunes at night, luring ships onto the shoals. Then they executed the survivors and plundered the wreckage.

Now their scion was setting tables for a New York Irishman. Ida's father raised vegetables in a patch in the mangrove swamps, hidden where passing boats couldn't raid it. He trapped lobsters for sale to Ryan and to a Miami restaurateur who flew in on a seaplane once a week. Ida's brother Sandy dove for turtles, sold the meat to Ryan, and shellacked the huge patterned shells for sale to visiting yachtsmen. He also did repairs around the inn in his soiled Harley Davidson T-shirt and tight Levi's. Like the other cay inhabitants, he was almost albino, with pale blue eyes and hair bleached white by the sun.

Ryan felt a bond with these simple people. Their lives, pared down by necessity to the essentials, possessed an inherent dignity. He was proud to have cast his lot with them. He found himself gazing at Ida's hips as she leaned across the table, maid's dress stretched taut. Stooping, he rearranged bottles beneath the bar.

"Mr. Ryan, you want the tables in here set, too?"

Ryan stood up. Ida rarely spoke. When she did, he was always startled by her cockney accent. It was harsh, in contrast to Ida's languid mannerisms. She strolled rather than walked, lolled rather than sat, had a slow, lazy smile. Like Henry Higgins in *My Fair Lady*, he wanted to correct her vowel sounds.

"I don't think we'll need them tonight."

All evening Ryan mixed daiquiris and planters' punches for yachtsmen from New York and Connecticut. The men wore pressed white trousers, deck shoes or Reeboks, striped T-shirts, white captain's hats. They had clipped mustaches and styled hair. The women wore caftans or pants suits. Long painted nails, eye makeup, careful coiffures. Bronzed by the sun. The beautiful people. They shrieked with laughter, clinked the ice cubes in their glasses, and ordered too many refills, just as he, Elaine, and the Achesons had done three years earlier. This former self seemed foreign to Ryan now. He answered the guests' friendly questions curtly, feeling like a reformed alcoholic who must avoid all contact with his poison.

A Connecticut captain shouldered his way to the bar and leaned on it. "Some place, this Conch Cay. Just like Hemingway, huh?"

Ryan nodded, not looking up.

"How'd you find it anyhow?"

"Same as you," muttered Ryan, shaking a margarita in a silver container. "Sailing around on vacation." Every yachtsman who stopped here regarded the cay as his private discovery.

"Where you from? I can hear you're not native."

"Manhattan." Ryan wished the guy would go back to his boat and stick his head in his chemical toilet.

"Threw it all up for the simple life, huh?"

"Something like that."

"Jesus, I envy you. To turn your back on the rat race. Just pack it in. Man oh man. How'd you do it?"

Ryan shrugged. "I just did it."

"Christ, you must have a pair and a half!" whistled the florid-faced captain as he moved away.

Ryan smiled grimly, since he hadn't been able to get it up for the last year. He could hear this man at a Westport cocktail party: "Lillian and I discovered this great little island. Gorgeous pink beaches. Mile after mile with nobody around. And right in the middle of nowhere, an inn with fabulous native cooking, run by this ballsy guy from Manhattan...." And next year half of Westport would arrive on Conch. Ryan's living depended on these people, but he didn't want them to come. He didn't like the way the men's eyes moved down Ida's body, the way they tossed coins to Sandy for carrying their bags from the ferry. He should be protecting the islanders from people like this instead of making his living off them.

Ryan's gaze sought out Ida, in her white uniform serving these impossible people. A woman had just sent something back to the kitchen. Ryan felt sure from Ida's tolerant smile that she could see through all their blustery pretension.

Ida was excited as she carried a turtle steak back to the kitchen for more cooking. She loved these attractive, well-dressed continental people, the way they demanded that everything be done exactly right—requesting clean glasses if there were water spots, clean forks if theirs were flecked with food. At her own house it was a miracle if an official meal ever happened, never mind how it was cooked. Her mother washed clothes all morning in cold water from the cistern, then sat around all afternoon munching Cracker Jacks and watching soap operas on the Miami station. At suppertime each of them would fix a bowl of Captain Crunch or go to the store for a Dolly Madison cake and a Coke.

Ida studied the woman whose turtle steak she was returning. A floral caftan, gold filigree on her wrists, emerald pendants hanging from her ears. A high black hairdo. Just like the models in the copies of *Vogue* guests sometimes left behind in their rooms. Ida sighed. They came and they went, these people, but she was stuck forever on this boring little island. Her life was all mapped out for her. Day after day, year after year, she would do the exact same things—change sheets, wait on tables, go for a ride after supper in Ben's boat, go into Orono for a movie, watch the soaps on TV. She would probably marry Ben, have babies, wash diapers all morning in cold water.

Once Ida had taken the ferry to Orono and the plane to Miami, to visit an aunt who had managed to escape. Fancy cars, tall glass office buildings, hotels with huge trees growing inside them. Men in suits and ties, something she had never seen except on TV and in the copies of *Gentlemen's Quarterly* guests left behind. What she couldn't figure out was why people like them voluntarily came to Conch Cay when they could go anywhere in the world—Paris or Rio or Disney World. And why they paid more money than she earned in an entire day to eat conch and turtle when they could be eating Big Macs instead.

There had to be a way out of this place. Once four men invited her onto their yacht. All day long she did everything they wanted. Some of it hurt, but she thought if she could please them, they would take her to Miami, as they had promised. Instead they dumped her at the far end of the island. She walked home barefoot over the coral. Her feet got all cut up. Sandy went looking for them. He washed ashore in his boat the next day, unconscious, ribs broken and face bruised.

Looking up, Ida caught Mr. Ryan staring at her again. He had come to Conch Cay and meant to stay. From New York City. All by himself. On purpose. Said he liked it here. He was always staring at her, then looking away when she caught him. But he never did more than look. He seemed like a nice man. He never pinched her as she walked by. She liked his auburn hair streaked with gray, liked his sad green eyes, liked to picture him in his New York City suit and tie.

Ryan spent his days buying fish and vegetables from the islanders, answering mail about rates and dates, dealing with the perpetual water shortage, going to Orono in his boat to pick up guests and supplies. At night he ran the bar. He was busier than he had ever been on Madison Avenue. But he was healthy and happy. His hair was bleaching in the sun, and he was tanned a reddish brown. He had stopped smoking and drinking. The whites of his eyes, always bloodshot in New York, were clear now.

His only source of agitation was Ida. Ryan watched her from his office window one morning as she moved slowly from room to room in the long low building across the yard. Her uniform dress stretched tight across her hips or breasts as she bent, stooped, and shook out rugs in the white sunlight. Unable to stop himself, Ryan pictured her naked beneath him on a deserted beach, tongues of frothy surf licking away their sweat.

He smiled sadly. His lechery was strictly pro forma. That phase of his life, in which his stiff penis had propelled him into all kinds of delicious disasters, was over now. He might as well resign himself to a dignified old age. He would become wise instead. Ida would come to him for advice. He would be a refuge from all the other men who wanted only sex. She was so innocent. He wouldn't want to contaminate her with lusts learned from a dying civilization, even if he could.

"Mr. Ryan, *sir*." Ryan discovered Sandy watching him watch Ida. "Would you radio Orono and order me half a dozen two-by-fours for the porch roof on the next ferry?"

"Uh, certainly, Sandy."

Arlene Dominique had been coming to the inn for years, she told Ryan as he dined at her table that night. He nodded, sipping his turtle soup. He disliked this woman, as an individual and as a type. She was like Elaine, like all the pampered, spoiled women he had ever known, in her low-cut sundress, gold sandals, jade eye shadow, Opium perfume, with strategic chunks of gold and diamond at ears, neck, and wrists. But she was an old-timer, belonged on Conch Cay more than he did. He had to be polite.

"...and then my husband died. That was two years ago. I've come back to Conch alone both years. It's therapeutic. Herb and I were so happy here. I talk to the natives about him. It's balm on my wounds to hear the wonderful things these simple souls have to say about my poor Herbie."

Ryan nodded with what he hoped was a sympathetic expression.

"But I'm a man's woman, Mr. Ryan." She looked at him through lowered eyelashes, heavy with crumbs of mascara. "I feel only half alive without a man."

It hadn't occurred to Ryan that sex was a service he was expected to provide, along with fresh linens. Ida's hip brushed his arm. She had been silently bringing new dishes and taking away soiled ones. Ryan looked up with a long-suffering smile and was met by an icy glare. She stalked to the kitchen with the soup plates.

"She's lovely, isn't she?" Mrs. Dominique noted his eyes following Ida's hips. "So innocent. A child really. I've known her since she was five. A darling little girl. And such a nice family. A real comfort to me after Herb's death."

Ryan nodded, grimly flaking yellowfish from its bones.

"But of course sympathy doesn't remedy certain needs associated with widowhood, Mr. Ryan. After eighteen years of constant physical contact with a man, a woman can't just suddenly turn it off at the funeral..."

A plate of chowder flipped off Ida's tray into Mrs. Dominique's lap. The dining room erupted—Mrs. Dominique shrieking, Ida mopping at her lap with a napkin, Ryan stuttering apologies. Mrs. Dominique retired to her room, scalded and outraged.

Ryan found Ida hiding in the pantry. "You have to be more careful, Ida," he began. "Mrs. Dominique has been coming here a long time, and sending her friends here. I know it was an accident, but it's one we can't afford."

She looked up, eyes red and puffy. "I'm sorry."

"It's all right. Please don't cry about it."

"I'm not."

"Not what?"

"Not crying about the chowder."

"What's wrong, then?"

"Nothing," she said sullenly.

Ida guessed she was in love with Ryan. It was hard to say since she had never been in love before. She had had boyfriends, but they were just that—boys who were special friends. Ben, the current one, drove his boat every day to a nearby cay to build condominiums. She had known him from infancy; knew his parents, grandparents, brothers and sisters; was some kind of cousin to him; knew exactly what their marriage would be like before it even began. She liked Ben fine, but there was no mystery. She didn't feel about him the way Laura did about Brad on *The Young and the Restless*, for instance, trembling when he walked in the room.

Ryan, however, did give her tremors. She thought about him all the time as she changed sheets and scoured toilet bowls, as she set tables and wrote orders, as she walked along the sand sidewalks late at night to her parents' house on the far side of the cove, as she lay in bed and listened to the wind drive the palm fronds together like clashing swords.

She liked to picture him in New York City—tall, slim, sophisticated, dressed in a pinstriped suit. She imagined meeting him for cocktails in a fancy hotel, riding to the roof in an open glass elevator. She would wear an Indian print caftan, jewels, mauve eye shadow, and a high hairdo with a spit curl at each ear. They would gaze at each other without speaking and toy with their plastic swizzle sticks. Then he would take her to a room with wall-to-wall carpeting, thick drapes, and a marble sink, where you could run water day and night without the cistern's ever going dry. On a huge bed with a quilted spread she would do all the things she had learned from the passing yachtsmen. And Ryan would insist she never leave.

Ida buried her face in her hands and wept. How was she to get to a bed in a New York hotel from a barrel in a pantry on Conch Cay? How could she compete with someone like Arlene Dominique? She couldn't. Ryan would go tonight to Aunt

Arlene (as Ida had been instructed by her parents to call the bitch years ago so the Christmas checks would keeping coming), and Aunt Arlene would do those things to him, and he would love her and go away with her, leaving Ida to rot on Conch Cay.

Later that night Ida sat sniffling in the bushes to one side of Ryan's door, waiting to watch him sneak to Aunt Arlene's room, while the generators clanked and the palm fronds clashed and mating cats yowled in the swamp. But dawn eventually streaked the night sky with dove gray and pink, and still Ryan hadn't appeared.

Aunt Arlene's door opened. Dressed in a long brown satin dressing gown, she strode back and forth along the porch smoking a cigarette. Finally she threw it down and marched to Ryan's door. She paused there, then whirled around and stalked back to her own room. Ida wiped away her tears with her dingy white uniform skirt.

As she served Ryan breakfast in his office that morning, she said, "Mr. Ryan, you work too hard. I bet you've never even seen Coral Cove."

"I've never even heard of it."

"We could go there this afternoon. After I finish the rooms."

Ryan hesitated. She was right, of course. He was working harder than was really necessary. He swam in the ocean every day for relaxation, but he hadn't yet toured his new island home. He studied Ida's eager face. She was Jessica's age. Was he a father figure? Was Ida a devoted employee trying to ingratiate herself with the boss? Was she lonely too, and wanting a new friend? Or was she propositioning him?

He smiled, realizing he was flattering himself to think that such an attractive young woman would be interested sexually in a graying old man. He had spotted her around the village with various young studs—the white-haired, red-faced, blue-eyed youth whom it was impossible to tell apart. She probably had a boyfriend. She was just being hospitable.

"I'd like to. That sounds like fun."

They walked under the white-hot sun along the pink sand for several miles. Ryan wore tennis shorts and carried their picnic hamper. Ida wore a two-piece bathing suit and a large straw hat with a gingham band. The surf swirled around their ankles. Periodically they squatted to inspect some object washed up by the waves—slimy, convoluted green noodle lasagnas, a Portuguese man-of-war like an inflated blue condom.

"How come there are never any village people on the beaches?" asked Ryan.

"When you grow up here, you don't think about the beach. My mother hasn't been over here in years."

"But do you all realize how unbelievably beautiful it is?"

Ida shrugged.

They were passing a ruined house, roof missing, walls crumbling, lush tropical bushes pushing up through the tile floors. Vines wound in and out the window openings like boa constrictors.

"Someone's house?" asked Ryan.

"Mr. Norton's. The continental who owned the inn before you."

"What happened?"

"Burnt down."

"Fires must be a real problem here once they get going," mused Ryan. "No rain, no roads, no fire-fighting equipment, no water except the ocean."

Ida nodded.

Coral Cove was pink sand on one side. Along the far side, coral formations in shades of black, mauve, and blood red shimmered in the heat. They spread a blanket, ate sandwiches, ran in and out of the water, and baked in the hot sun. Ryan watched Ida's breasts bouncing as she leapt into the waves. And her long brown legs stretched along the olive army blanket. He concentrated on thinking of her as his daughter, an innocent young woman entrusted to his protection. Not that Jessica had been innocent since she was two years old. But it was pointless to think of Ida any other way. If he did, and if she responded with anything other than horror, he would only disappoint them both.

Handing Ryan a mango from the hamper, Ida felt confused. This man was unlike any other male she had ever met. It had always been a question of fighting them off. But now she found herself wanting one who apparently wasn't interested. Maybe he was shy. What if she reached over and took his hand? But what if he really wasn't interested in her that way? What about her job? She thought men couldn't manage for very long without shoving themselves into some woman. That's what passing sailors and the boys on the cay always told her. Did Ryan have someone else? But he never left the island except to pick up arriving guests, and he hadn't gone to Aunt Arlene last night. She had heard there were men who wanted other men. Maybe he was one of those? She bit into her orange-fleshed mango, juice coursing down her chin.

"Mr. Ryan?"

He turned to look at her, mouth and hands mango-wet.

"Mr. Ryan, do you like me?"

"I like you very much, Ida."

"Do you like me—that way?"

"Which way?" he asked nervously.

Tossing her mauled mango into the surf, Ida rolled over and pressed her body against his. Ryan drew a sharp breath. They began to entangle juice-coated limbs and to kiss stickily, stirring up sand that clung to their moist skin.

Abruptly Ryan rolled on his back and stared at the blue sky. This young woman whose innocence he had pledged himself to protect had been writhing against him like a lady wrestler. She seemed to know exactly what she was doing. And his hands had taken on a life of their own, running up and down her curves. He felt ashamed of himself and betrayed by her. Some of her moves involved gymnastics described in the sex manuals Elaine had taken to leaving on his bedside table before they split up. Perverse gimmicks dreamed up by a sick civilization to flog response out of zombies in whom all spontaneity was dead. The more demands Elaine made, the more she chronicled his failures, and the more she outlined techniques for "satisfying" her, the less he was able to sustain an erection. How did a young girl on a remote island know about such repulsive behavior? If his role weren't to be her guardian, at least *he* should be the one to instruct *her* in lovemaking.

"You don't want to—love me?" asked Ida, bewildered.

"It's not that simple."

Ida felt panic. She wasn't pleasing Ryan. She didn't know how the sophisticated women he was used to behaved. With Ben it was enough simply to lie down, open her legs, and think about *The Young and the Restless* until he was finished. But the men on the boats expected more exotic things. She recalled a scene from a late-night movie on TV. Climbing atop Ryan, she ran her tongue around and into his ear, and sucked his lobe. "But it *is* simple, my darling," she whispered. "So simple."

Ryan shoved her off, leaped up, grabbed the blanket and basket, and stalked off toward the village.

"But I only want to please you, Mr. Ryan," she wailed, trotting alongside. "Just tell me how."

He stomped along wordlessly, past the ruined house of his predecessor.

"Please, Mr. Ryan. God, I love you so much."

He stopped and whirled around, glaring at her, outraged. Love? The only time he had ever said, "I love you" to someone, he ended up with two spoiled children, a mortgaged house in Darien, loans on a Volvo station wagon and a Honda Accord, a wife who was a compulsive shopper, a job writing lies, and a limp prick. He could tell this child of nature a thing or two about "love"! But when he noticed her tearstained face, he remembered she was hardly more than a teenager.

"You love me?"

"So much."

"You don't know what love means."

"It means that I want to be close to you."

"That's not all it means. And you're too young to know about the rest."

"I don't care. Please," she said, holding out her arms. They embraced gingerly, then walked to the village in silence, sand fleas feasting on their ankles.

For several days Ryan avoided Ida. He didn't know how to behave anymore. On the one hand, she was an innocent who had to be protected from himself. On the other hand, with her abandoned writhing on the beach, she represented some sort of primal sinkhole against which he had to protect *himself*. And yet he had experienced no physical warmth in a long time. He craved it. Here was an attractive young woman who claimed she loved him. Was it possible his notion of love was askew, shaped as it had been in the molds of a corrupt civilization?

Late one night after the last sailor returned to his yacht, Ida slipped into Ryan's room, out of her white uniform, and into his bed. He moaned and held her close. They lay without talking in each other's arms until dawn.

Ida was startled. She hadn't known how to act, had known only that her behavior at Coral Cove had not been a hit. So she decided to make herself available to him to do with as he wanted. What he apparently wanted was just to lie with her, occasionally brushing back her hair and kissing her forehead. What an odd man. Was this really how New Yorkers had sex?

136

All the stuff the men on the boats made her do must have been saved for vacations.

This went on for several weeks. Ryan became more and more reassured. They had just gotten off to a bad start. He had misinterpreted a healthy young girl's innate enthusiasm for sex as corruption. She merely happened to be still in touch with the natural tides of her own body. He had projected his own sickness onto her, the contagion that had led him to regard sex as an exchange—the woman consenting in return for material support from the man. The sun, the sea, the wind, the preparation of food and shelter—might there be a place in this natural cycle for a kind of lovemaking he had never imagined, lovemaking that could salve his loneliness without dragging PTA meetings in its wake, a melding and merging rather than a commercial transaction?

In the course of such musings one night, while Ida snuggled against him playing with the springy red hairs on his chest, Ryan felt a swelling in his groin. He lay still, waiting for it to subside, but it didn't.

In the ensuing months, Ryan experienced things he hadn't known were possible between two people. He felt both resentful and apologetic toward Elaine. Resentful because she had been content for so many years with a tepid counterfeit of lovemaking, despite her self-portrayal as a slighted courtesan. Apologetic because he hadn't given her this kind of pleasure, hadn't even known it existed. Possibly it didn't exist in Darien. He suspected it required the stripping off of material obsession and cultural conditioning he had undergone on Conch. Perhaps it required a partner in a similar state of simplicity.

Whatever, every minute Ryan and Ida weren't working, they were in bed together, discovering and inventing new ways to give each other pleasure. Never had he felt more virile. Ida was constantly praising his revived member. In between demanding to be told about New York City, block by block, building by building.

"You must look so handsome in a suit," she kept insisting.

"I promise you I look better without one."

"No, Ryan, I can just picture you," she sighed, closing her eyes.

One afternoon they were lying in each other's arms on the deserted pink beach, the surf licking their legs. The shell of the burnt-out house was keeping watch behind them.

Ida whispered, "Ryan, I have something to tell you." She paused, unsure how he would react. "I'm going to have your baby."

Ryan said nothing. At first, he felt strangely proud. He, a graying old man, had impregnated this gorgeous young woman. And after all, it was right that a union as simple and natural as theirs should come to this. But he had been through it all before—diapers, toilet training, teething, braces, piano recitals. He had done the parenting trip for all time. He wanted nothing more to do with it. No, it was out of the question. Ida would have an abortion. He would take her to Miami.

"That's wonderful," he said faintly.

"Do you really think so?" She took his hand and ran it over her swelling belly. He would marry her, take her away from this awful place.

"Sure. Great." He could climb in his boat in the morning, be in Miami before noon, sell the inn by proxy, send Ida money.

"Ryan, I'm so happy to have your baby growing inside me."

That night Ryan sat in the yard under the rattling palms and downed half a bottle of brandy. Time after time he ran through his options—abortion, flight, suicide, marriage. In that order of desirability. Abortion made the most sense. He would take Ida to Miami, have it over with before anyone on the island even knew about it. Take her to a fancy hotel for a few days to cheer her up.

But she was so pleased to be pregnant. She had no children, hadn't experienced the drudgery of rearing them. The abortion, if she agreed to it, would be a trauma. How could he have been so stupid as not to think about birth control? Elaine and the other women he had been with had always taken care of it. But how could he expect an innocent like Ida to know about it, much less have access to it. Besides, it would have seemed a sacrilege to impose a rubber shield or a plunger of foam between them.

Sandy staggered out of the bushes, drunk. The spotlights illuminating the palms bathed his body in white and reduced his face to eerie shadows. "Got summin I wanna tell ya, Ryan."

"What, Sandy?" he asked wearily.

"You do right by my sister, mon."

Ryan stared at him, horrified. Ida had already told her family? "Why don't you mind your own goddamn business?"

"Fuck you, Ryan! You been balling my sister all over this bloody island and everybody knows it! You do right by her, mon, or I'll cut your goddamn balls off!"

Ryan leapt to his feet. "Shut up, you maniac! You're going to wake up the whole damn place!"

Sandy swung at him and missed. They ended up lying on the ground passing the brandy bottle and exchanging life histories. Sandy's voice oozed hatred as he described how the visiting yachtsmen came on shore and acted as if they owned the cay, stealing vegetables from his father's garden, knocking up the local girls, beating up the boys and taking lobsters from their traps.

"And some of them even come back here to live," said Sandy, apparently forgetting whom he was talking to. "They think this island's so fucking beautiful. And they act like we're just turds who happen to have washed ashore. But they don't last long."

"What do you mean?" Ryan felt himself sobering up quickly.

"Quality control, mon."

"Norton's burnt house," Ryan realized.

Sandy grinned slyly. "Ain't saying nothing 'bout no burnt house, Ryan." He thrust the bottle at him, and Ryan took a long gulp.

Early the next morning Ryan climbed in his boat. He had errands on Orono. But he might be on the afternoon flight to Miami, watching from the air as his abandoned inn went up in flames. Abortion was probably out. Ida's family was Primitive Baptist. They would never allow it. If Ida were dumb enough to tell them, she could cope with the consequences alone.

Steering his Boston Whaler out of the harbor, he turned to follow the shoreline. It wasn't that he didn't love Ida, insofar as he knew what that word meant. It was just that he had been through all this before with Elaine, knew how devotion turned into duty, and duty into dislike. It was better to end it while it was still perfect. He was doing them both a favor.

As he passed the shoals, a large speedboat swept up, nosed toward him, and forced him sharply shoreward.

"What the fuck!" he screamed. His boat lurched, throwing him into the dashboard. He heard a sickening crunch as his keel ran aground on the coral. There was a sharp pain in his chest.

Looking up, he saw Sandy, idling his boat in the nearby water. "Remember what I said, Ryan. Do right by my sister, mon, or you'll wish you had." His boat roared away.

Ryan shut off his grinding engine, climbed onto the reef, and inspected the damage. A hole in the hull. The boat was done for. The motor could maybe be saved. He waded and swam to shore over the shoals where Ida's ancestors had looted wrecked ships. Then he hiked back to the village along the pink sand beach where he and Ida had first kissed, past the vine-wrapped ruins. The physical pain in his chest began to subside, only to be replaced by despair. There was no way to get off this island alive without Ida. Everyone on it was related to her. Maybe a passing yacht would rescue him?

As he reached the wooden stairs over the dunes to the village, he came upon the Baptist minister, who wore a handkerchief, knotted at each corner, on his balding head. A Canadian, he had come to Conch as a missionary forty years earlier and never left. He held a dried palm frond in one hand, with which he had printed in the sand, "The Lord Has a Plan for Your Life." The rising tide was eating its edges. He started as Ryan greeted him.

Ryan pointed to the eroding message. "Do you really think so, Reverend?"

"I know so," replied the old man, gazing at Ryan through crazed blue eyes.

That night in bed Ida whispered, "Ryan, our baby is moving!" She placed his hand on her abdomen, and he felt the tiny shiftings. But he had done this with Elaine twice already. The experience had lost its power to enchant. He was instead calculating that it had to be about four months old, too late for a simple abortion. A saline abortion would be necessary. Ida would miscarry a dead fetus.

"Ida. I don't want a baby. I've had two already. I thought we could go to Miami. You could have an abortion. Then we could stay in a fancy hotel for a few days. Order from room service. The works. We'll tell your parents you miscarried."

Ida said nothing for a long time. Finally she replied, "Abortion is a sin."

"Oh, come on. Don't be ridiculous. Millions of women have abortions every year."

"That doesn't make it right."

"But Ida, I liked things the way they were."

Perhaps abortion *was* a sin? In any case, it was to Ida and her family. She was an innocent he had pledged to protect from the barbarities of modern civilization, and here he was asking her to murder her fetus. The whole situation seemed unreal. He was playing in a different league on Conch Cay and hadn't even realized it.

Ida wept and called him godless. As he held her, patted her, and felt awful, he wondered if, just as sex with Ida had been a totally new experience, rearing a child on Conch Cay might not be different from rearing one in Darien. What was one more kid on this island? He would marry Ida and move her in with him, hire a new waitress. Ida would have the baby, tend it. The little kid would run free in the sun and the sea. It might be beautiful. He shouldn't impose his warped view. All right, he concluded, he would become a father again.

The next morning as Ida and Ryan walked on the sand sidewalk around the cove to announce to her parents their impending marriage, they passed the one-room schoolhouse. Ryan took a close look. This was where his child would be educated. Baby Ruth wrappers swirled around their feet. They waded through Cracker Jack boxes and Coke bottles. Most of the children screaming in the playground were cousins to his incubating child. Their teeth were black. Several had crossed eyes. He walked on, feeling uneasy. It was different from how Jessica and Kevin had grown up, with their Montessori nursery school, but that didn't make it worse.

Ida, too, studied the children on the playground. Ryan wouldn't allow his child to grow up on Conch Cay with privies and cisterns, no phones, mail boats once a week, no high school. It was merely a matter of time until he would take her and their child away. She was sure of it.

Ida and Ryan looked at each other and smiled warily.

Ryan sat in the cocktail lounge of their Miami honeymoon hotel absently clinking the ice in his scotch. Ida stood in the doorway watching him. A frown creased her forehead. Ryan looked uncomfortable in his suit, kept stretching his neck against his tight collar and tie. His hair was bleached almost white by the sun, and his face was dark red. He looked like the Conch Cay men instead of the GQ models. Ida struggled to put on her brightest smile.

Ryan looked up and saw Ida sweeping toward him in a floral silk caftan, her swelling belly breaking the flowing lines. She had had her hair done—piled high on her head with spit curls at each ear. Gold bracelets clanked on her wrists.

"Well?" she demanded, demurely lowering mauve eyelids.

"You look lovely," Ryan assured her with a bemused smile.

BIRDMAN AND THE DANCER

At the tip of Manhattan, like a space-age Avebury, stands a
cluster of steel structures that channel the winter gusts off
Upper New York Bay and block out the summer sun. Within
their walls are determined the price of rice in Quito and the
number of Nissans produced in Nagoya. One semi-circular
building of glass looms over Battery Park, reflecting the clouds
and the shifting hues of the maples down below. At dawn,
seagulls in flight flit across its glass face, and at sunset its
smooth surface mirrors the molten sky.

A bond trader named Kostas Powers used to sit in this
building all day long, keeping track of the market on his
desktop monitor. At the close of each trading day, Kostas
walked five miles on the treadmill at his health club before
returning to Great Neck to eat dinner, watch videos of film
classics, and fall asleep beside Penelope, his wife of twenty-five
years, mother of his grown son Mike. On weekends Kostas ate
brunch at the butcher-block table in his kitchen, with its view
through a grove of sailboat masts across Manhasset Bay to
Sands Point. He did household repairs and yard work,
followed by a sail with Penny, then cocktails or dinner with
other couples in their set.

Kostas had been groomed for this life ever since his
Queens boyhood by a father who sold hair-care products to
beauty parlors. His father was determined that Kostas
complete the ascent into the American upper middle class
begun by his own father, Ippocrates Papaioias, who arrived in
America with only the contents of two wooden steamer trunks
to his name (a name he promptly changed to Ippocrates
Powers). Kostas could just barely remember the old man with

dark eyes like ripe olives and a head of sea-foam hair, whose hands smelled permanently of spoiled fish.

Sitting at his desk one afternoon studying bond prices as they danced their usual tarantella, Kostas heard a loud thud. He looked up to discover that a gull had been hurled against his window by a blast of wind off the bay. The gull, clouded eyes fluttering shut, was sliding down the pane, leaving a trail of blood. Watching the beak gasp for air, Kostas felt dread seep like swamp gas into his vitals. He stood up and walked to the window. With his fingertips he traced the powdery silhouette of outspread wings as the bird fell away from the window and hurtled toward the pavement.

Feeling panic, as though his office were a prison cell that reeked with his own sweat while he awaited the approaching guards, Kostas gazed across the bare maples in the park below, silver in the winter sun, to a ferry carrying tourists to the Statue of Liberty, lichen-green on her pedestal of stone, with the Victorian excesses of Ellis Island like a Turkish seraglio in the background. On Ellis Island, where the Hudson flows into Upper New York Bay, the trajectory that had landed Kostas in this glass high-rise had commenced. He had often stood in this same spot and imagined Ippocrates, refugee from a stony Aegean island, watching from the deck as his ship negotiated the Verrazano Narrows and headed towards the future site of Kostas's building, which nearly shadowed the fish market where Ippocrates had scaled haddock for four decades. Kostas had always felt proud to have realized his grandfather's dream. This day, however, he did not feel proud. He felt frightened, and he didn't know why. He tried to open the window for some fresh air, then recalled that it was permanently sealed.

Later that afternoon, Kostas switched on the treadmill at his health club and began to run, reflecting that if the club would hook its exercise equipment to a generator, it could fuel lower Manhattan. After eight miles, tee shirt plastered to his chest, bad knee from a college basketball collision aching, Kostas climbed into the whirlpool. As he poached, he studied the open empty locker of a man who had died of a heart attack on the Stairmaster the previous week. From the treadmill, Kostas had watched him cling oddly to the handgrips, as though about to perform a gymnastic stunt. Then his body contorted, and he appeared to hyperventilate. In his early forties, a former St. Lawrence hockey player, he had often exchanged fitness tips with Kostas in the sauna.

The night of Kostas's encounter with the dying gull, Penny lit two candles on one of Ippocrates' steamer trunks by the stone fireplace in their cathedral-ceilinged living room. She had refinished the trunk herself, painting the metal bands black and polishing the brass nail heads. From the kitchen she carried moussaka and a salad heaped high with black olives and goat cheese. They took pride in having bucked the trend of their generation, both embracing their traditional roles: Penny had stayed home to rear Mike and make of their home a castle for Kostas. Now that Mike was a psychology doctoral student at Princeton, Penny had developed a passion for Kostas's Greek heritage, so colorful in contrast to her own bland Boston Mayflower inheritance of baked beans and steamed brown bread. She laughingly called Kostas her "Greek god," which amused him because he had long since accepted the fact that, although pleasant looking, he was not handsome, with his receding chin, unruly cowlick, and pointed nose that had earned him the childhood nickname of The Beak.

Penny's new enthusiasm also amused him because Ippocrates had turned his back on everything Greek. Kostas had cousins in the City whom he had never met because Ippocrates had insisted that all Greeks were "backward." Ippocrates had prohibited his wife from cooking Greek dishes, and she had had to sneak out to Greek Orthodox services. He had often demanded in his broken English why would he have come to America if he had wanted "all that Greek claptrap." ("Claptrap" was his favorite English word.) He named his firstborn son George, not after the famous dragon-slaying saint so cherished by his homeland, but after George Washington. He encouraged George to marry a WASP. The best George could do was a tall Irish Catholic, from whom Kostas had acquired his basketball-star physique and his dreamy malamute eyes. It had almost destroyed Ippocrates when George had insisted on naming *his* firstborn Constantine and calling him Kostas. Ippocrates had always called Kostas "Stan."

"What's wrong, darling?" asked Penny, pouring retsina.

"Nothing's wrong."

She raised her eyebrows.

"I was just thinking that we'd need about eight hundred of these trunks for our possessions. Yet Ippocrates arrived here with only two."

"True," said Penny, perplexed.

In bed Kostas hid himself in the warmth of Penny's arms. Theirs had been a real love match, and still was, though their definition of "love" had shifted over the years. At Yale Penny became an obsession for Kostas the moment she stepped off the bus from Connecticut College in her cashmere sweater set and tartan kilt, with WASP cheekbones that would have ravished Ippocrates. When Kostas discovered that she was his blind date, he knew there was a God. "Love" then meant being scarcely able to catch his breath as he dialed her dorm to invite her for a weekend. It meant being unable to stop gazing at her whenever she was in his presence. In time, love came to mean needing to touch some part of her body at all times, even in company, as though some vital fluid were being transferred between them. Eventually love meant the delight of purchasing their first sofa together, then the astonishment of cradling in his arms a screaming red infant who had just emerged from her body.

At this point their love entered its Dark Ages. Kostas, distraught that Penny seemed to prefer Mike to himself, allowed outsiders to rivet his attention, emergency flares in the breakdown lane of their love. Once he succumbed to these urges with a young broker who regarded him as her mentor. Kostas suspected Penny knew because he was a terrible liar, blushing and stammering when trying to explain why he was home late. But she had had the good grace to remain silent until this scow foundered and sank. Always, like scissors, however far apart he and Penny might appear, anyone who had come between them had gotten chopped up.

They had experienced the usual mutual eagerness for escape via divorce when Mike was a raging adolescent. But even this hurricane had moved offshore, and now they were enjoying the rewards for endurance. Once again there were extra hours for lolling in bed, and no threat of a young skinhead barging in with a blaring boom box and an endless litany of complaint about the outdated slang and wardrobes of his loathed parents. Penelope's breasts sagged, but so did Kostas's jowls, and they both had pouches of adipose below their waistlines. Penny had varicose veins on one calf, and Kostas had a lacy net of broken blood vessels on his pointed nose that made him look alcoholic. At Yale it was all Kostas could do, as he knelt over Penny struggling with a condom, to restrain himself until he got inside her, but now he could have lasted until Doomsday. What they had lost in excitement had been compensated for by tenderness. Kostas was familiar with each crease in Penny's body, knew in advance every endearment she would whisper, which caresses she would initiate when. In short, Kostas was a bit bored.

"What's wrong, honey?" whispered Penny, stroking his stubborn cowlick while a wind from the Sound whined outside their bedroom window.

"Nothing's wrong. Everything's right."

But the next morning as Kostas rode the elevator to his office, he found the anxiety from the previous afternoon gnawing his guts like a trapped rat. Walking into the bullpen where the secretaries and fledgling brokers sat, he felt sweat pop out on his upper lip and at his hairline. Some of the young people who were now greeting him often came into his office with tales of personal disaster and global woe, and he reassured them with all the wisdom of his half-century of life experience. It made him a good manager—apart from his skill at anticipating the syncopated rise and fall of different sectors of the market economy. But as he surveyed this roomful of hopeful faces, he realized there was nothing he could do to protect them from that hooded hangman who would eventually drag each off to some subterranean torture chamber for confessions and atonement. There was nothing he could do to protect himself from this. He smiled weakly at the attractive new temp from Vermont.

Pouring some coffee into the *Mr. Big* mug his secretary had given him, Kostas retreated to his office. Yet he had nothing to confess. He was a good boy who had grown up to be a nice guy. In Queens he had carried altar flowers to shut-ins, returned change to customers who overpaid him on his paper route, picked up broken glass in parking spaces. He had earned a full scholarship to Yale, where he had broken a long-standing basketball scoring record. This prowess on the court rendered many young women eager to sacrifice themselves on the altar of his manhood. He tried his best to decline these votive offerings, and when he failed, he protected the reputations of his deflowered devotees. As an adult, he always paid his taxes, contributed to the charities of his choice, and kept his cholesterol count below 200. Now, however, he was unable to evade a visceral knowledge that one day soon, because of some obscure crime, it would be his turn on the rack.

Puzzled, Kostas studied a framed photo on his walnut desk of Mike, Penny, and himself in front of the Christmas tree last month. In the picture, Kostas looked crazed because of having tripped while taking his place after setting the camera timer. Both Ippocrates and George had insisted that a man's job was to protect and provide for his family, and Kostas had always given Penny and Mike all the necessities and many of the luxuries. Whenever possible, he had interposed himself between them and potential danger. Yet at Christmas, over cups of eggnog around Ippocrates' chest, Mike said, "You coddled me, Dad."

"I did the best I could."

"You undermined me. It was nothing but a power trip."

"A Powers trip?" said Kostas, trying to restore an air of festivity.

"Fine, Dad. Always the *bon mot* whenever someone tries to say something serious around this place."

"Should I punch you instead?"

"Right. Murder the messenger who speaks unwelcome truths."

"Whatever." Kostas had sipped his eggnog despondently in the light of the flashing tree.

"I had so hoped," sighed Penny, "that we could finally get through a holiday without your needing to play Skewer Your Father, Mike."

Mike's neck and face turned a deep alizarin crimson. "All right, but one final question, Dad."

Kostas nodded resignedly.

"What's it all for?" He waved his hand around the room. "I can aspire to buying a fancier house, car, boat. But what's the point? You gave me everything I need except a reason to be alive rather than dead."

Kostas drew a deep breath. "I guess I never stopped working long enough to ask that. My grandfather arrived on a boat from Greece with the contents of two trunks and spent the rest of his life peeling shrimp, so that you can sit in this expensive house and tell me it was all pointless."

"But what if it was?"

What if it was? echoed a voice in Kostas's head as he studied Mike in his desk photo. What if the Papaioias family saga was nothing more than aimless island hopping—from Anafi to Ellis Island to Manhattan Island to Long Island? What if its sole result was to land Kostas here in this glass building with windows that wouldn't open, dressed in an Armani suit, fluctuating like the bond market between boredom and terror, until he got old and sick and died? Maybe this was his unfathomable crime—pointlessness? With growing unease he regarded the outline on his windowpane of the outspread wings of the colliding gull, backed by the roiling grey sky above the bay.

While the bond market continued its relentless rise and fall in response to real and imagined world events, Kostas's family doctor pronounced him in the grip of an anxiety attack and put him on Xanax. During the ensuing months, Kostas dragged Penny to the Catholic church of his boyhood every Sunday. He enrolled in an NYU night course on major world religions and learned that however their proposed solutions might differ, the bottom line for each was what his whimsical professor termed the four D's—disease, destruction, despair, and death. Determined not to be a wimp, Kostas attended weekends in the Berkshires at which professional men like himself argued over who was the most cooperative, painted their bare chests, and drummed and danced by the light of the harvest moon, searching for their lost tribal selves.

This floundering was not a comfortable stance for Kostas. On the basketball court, either a basket was scored or not. A math major at Yale, he was accustomed to right and wrong answers and had assiduously avoided humanities students, who seemed to pride themselves on ambivalence and angst. On the bond market a price rose or fell, you made a profit or took a loss. This endless uncertainty was new to him, and since he could define only the symptoms, he was unable to formulate a strategy for eliminating the cause. Finally, after months of soul-searching with a baffled Penny, Kostas sold off his portfolio, split the proceeds with Penny, purchased a round-the-world ticket on Northwest Orient, outdid Ippocrates by packing a few things in a knapsack, and kissed his bewildered wife farewell.

"Kostas, I love you," said Penny firmly as she dropped him off at Kennedy. "I know you've been having a hard time, and I'll try my best to wait for your return."

Kostas looked at the companion of all his adult years. "I love you too, Penny—and have loved you. But I don't know when I'll be back, so maybe you'd better find someone else."

"That's for me to decide."

So Kostas hit the road like Ippocrates before him, undergoing trials too numerous and tedious to detail. Suffice it to say that he wandered by the light of the rising sun, and the moon in all its phases. He traveled on land and on sea, over mountain peaks and through desert wastes. He watched in rain forests as wild beasts nursed their young, then ripped their prey to bits; in world capitols as citizens gave change to beggars, then beat their children behind drawn drapes. More and more he resembled those beggars as his Armani suit grew soiled and tattered, as hollows formed beneath his cheekbones, as his thinning hair turned greasy, as a graying beard concealed his recessed chin, as holes formed in the soles of his wing-tip shoes. People began to avert their eyes when they saw him coming, and they held their breath so as not to inhale his stench.

One night Kostas decided he should visit Anafi, birthplace of Ippocrates, an Odyssean homecoming that might finally teach him something or other. But the gods were as hostile to Kostas as to Odysseus: On a dock in Athens, as he attempted to stow away on an island-bound ferry, a gang of street boys attacked him, grunting and snarling like wild animals. At first he did his Rambo-best to fight them off. But when he glimpsed the glint of knives scarlet with his own blood, he heard a soothing yet authoritative female voice in his head: "Let go, Kostas. Give up. Give in." Obediently he sagged like a rag doll. As this vision of rising and falling fists, sticks and knives faded, Kostas was surprised to feel no pain, only an ineffable peace. Believing they had killed him, the boys fled.

An old man in a hooded brown robe, with a face like a dried apple, was spooning broth from a cup into Kostas's mouth. Patting all around himself with both hands, Kostas discovered that he was covered with bandages and was lying on a straw pallet on a dirt floor. The only light came from a single candle, and the walls appeared to be stone. The pain missing during the attack was now present.

"Where am I?" he managed to croak.

The man looked at him for a moment, spoon suspended, then resumed feeding him.

The man returned several times a day to bring rice and change dressings, and it became apparent that he couldn't speak. It also became apparent that Kostas's room was a cave. What was not apparent was whether Kostas was a guest or a captive. On some visits the old man's face seemed benign; on others, cunning and cruel. Had Kostas died during the attack?

Was the old man the executioner Kostas had dreaded from the heights of his glass office building? What if the Baptists were right about hell? Once his wounds healed, maybe a skewer would be inserted up his ass and he would become barbecue for the devil.

Eventually Kostas began to sit up and look around. His cave was clean and bare, apart from a colony of bats that inhabited the vaulted ceiling, whirling out of the cave mouth each evening at dusk. From the rear came the trickle and splash of water, though it was too dark to locate the source. There were no bars or doors across the opening. Once he could walk, he would find out what was outside, and whether or not he was free to leave.

Finally he was able to stand, basketball knee aching badly. And one day he regained enough balance to pull on the coarse brown robe by his pallet and take several shuffling steps. Gasping with pain, he sat back down, promising himself a trip to the cave mouth in the near future.

That torturous journey required what seemed like several hours, though since his watch had been stolen in the attack, Kostas couldn't be sure. On the treadmill he had sometimes timed himself to the second, but here he knew only if it were day or night, according to the light through the cave mouth.

Arriving at the opening, Kostas discovered a dirt path outside, overlooking a cliff of jagged rock that plunged hundreds of feet to a tangled swamp that was putrid with rotting vegetation and chartreuse slime. Across the sky lay a smear of sun like a bloody thumbprint.

Hesitantly, as though expecting alarm bells, he put one foot on the path, then the other. Nothing happened, so he took several more halting steps in the open air, blasted with a heat that the cave's coolness had been keeping at bay. Turning to face his cave, he learned that it was merely one among hundreds that pocked a mountain face that extended out of

sight overhead and on both sides. Paths wound up and down
the mountain, punctuated by steep steps of stone. No human
presence was discernible. Evidently Kostas could leave if he
wished, but there seemed nowhere to go.

Kostas never encountered the old man again. His bowls of
rice were now left on the outside path. At first he was relieved
to be rid of the mad monk. But then he began to miss him and
to feel remorse for having vilified him. But how had Kostas
arrived here? Had he come on his own during a bout of
amnesia? Yet he had been half-dead and could never have
scaled that jagged rock wall by himself.

Tracing the splashing noise to the rear of his chamber,
Kostas discovered an underground stream that roiled with
albino crayfish. At the far end it disappeared into the
mountain. From the damp ceiling hung hosts of stalactites, like
the roots of giant molars. One day he followed for what felt
like miles the twisting footpaths and stone steps that stitched
the mountain face, passing cave mouths with no one inside.
But he never reached a point from which he could see anything
other than the mountain and the swamp.

Most of the time he merely sat in his doorway and
watched winged carnivores down below skewer sluggish fish
on their shiny black beaks. And the stir of snarled vines as
giant snakes slithered through the stagnant water, their dark
scales glistening green and blue and red as fingers of golden
sun poked through the banks of royal purple storm clouds
overhead.

What began as an acceptable solitude shaded off into
unease, then into full-blown loneliness. For company he took
to playing with the white crayfish, naming them and trying to
interest them in grains of rice. One day it occurred to him that
he could liven up his diet with one of his pale crustacean pals.
Salivating, he imagined boiling water in his cup over his
candle and holding a crayfish under, as he had often done to

lobsters back home. As he pictured smashing a crayfish with a rock and eating it raw, he realized that he was losing his mind, since the crayfish were currently his only companions.

Recalling from a course at Yale that soldiers who fared best in prison camps were those who developed a regimen of physical and mental exercise, he began doing calisthenics on his cave floor to recondition his flaccid muscles. Then he would sit in his doorway and summarize from his NYU course the attitudes of the different world religions toward life on earth— the indifference of the Buddhists, the disgust of the Christians and Moslems, the Hindu insistence on illusion. He decided to reconstruct day by day, hour by hour, his entire life history, and then evaluate the interpretations of the various faiths, as though rating a bond offering. What religion needed was a systematic survey that exhibited all the clarity and precision of an algebraic formula, and Kostas was the man for the job.

But at night Kostas's regimen failed him, and he was assaulted by loneliness as though by the Athens street gang. Although he didn't really miss the "claptrap" of his Great Neck life, he did miss the people, for he was a team player, a family man, an urban creature, not a solitary philosopher. He would wrap his arms across his chest and pretend he was holding Penny. He talked to her out loud, describing the antics of the crayfish, the configurations of the storm clouds, the sleeping arrangements of the bats. One night when the agony was almost unbearable and he was considering leaping into the swamp as a snack for the lurking reptiles, he heard the woman's voice from the night of his attack: "Let go, Kostas. Give up. Give in." He obeyed—and was borne up on a swell of well-being.

The next night, and for many nights thereafter, Kostas struggled to give up, so that he could again experience that rush of soothing calm. But nothing happened. Recalling that some prisoners at Auschwitz had tried to preserve their sanity

by meeting regularly in their rags alongside the barbed wire
fence for an imaginary Viennese banquet, he decided to try to
imagine the woman who would possess such a caressing yet
commanding voice. Why not hold her in his arms and recount
his day? Surely Penny would agree that he deserved some
variety, given his present predicament.

The exact configurations of the woman were obscure
because she was wrapped in a caftan with a veil concealing her
face. But she was younger than Penny. The veins on the backs
of Penny's hands stood out like those on an autumn leaf, but
this woman's hands were smooth and soft. Housework, yard
work, and diaper pails had not yet exacted their toll.

Kostas felt ridiculous, a grown man inventing an
imaginary playmate. Pulling his robe over his shoulders, he
extinguished this fantasy and fell asleep. Though he was
increasingly less certain what was sleep, dream, or reality.
From then on, however, after the light through the cave mouth
had turned violet and flamingo, after the bats had swirled out
on their nightly foray, Kostas would lie on his pallet and
summon this young woman into his head, her specifications
becoming clearer little by little. Tall and graceful, she looked a
bit like Kostas had at her age, with the same unruly cowlick,
odd nose, and slim build. But where his body had been hard-
packed muscle, hers was smooth curves. As he regaled her
with fragments of his autobiography, she snuggled against his
chest and looked up at him admiringly.

Kostas had given this woman life, and he began to long to
give her much more—his protection, his body, his baby. He
yearned to search the swamp to find her treats, and to fight the
snakes to keep her safe. With horror, he understood that he
was falling in love with a figment of his own imagination. Yet
he found himself unable to renounce this idiocy because he
was so forlorn without it.

One morning Kostas sat contemplating a freshly spun spider web in a corner of his doorway, pleased to have a new neighbor, one with a handsome scarlet and gamboge hourglass on her shiny black back. The web was already studded with several emerald green flies, and it shimmered like mica as the spider briskly wrapped one of her guests in silky strands.

Kostas realized he was not alone. Standing above him holding his bowl of rice was the young woman. She wore an oyster-colored gown of striped silk that clung about her hips, abdomen, and breasts. She studied him as he sat with his mouth agape.

"Soup's on." She handed him his bowl. "*Bon appetit.*"

"Who are you?" Kostas managed to ask.

"Oh, Kostas, you know who I am." She laughed.

"Where did you come from?"

"You know that as well as I do."

Her voice was identical to the one he had heard in his head in Athens and since. "Are you actually real?"

"Do I seem real to you?"

He nodded, wondering if he had finally lost his mind.

"If you believe I'm real, then I'm real, no?"

"No," he agreed. "Uh, yes. I don't know."

Cocking her head this way and that, she said, "Stand up a minute, will you?"

Dazed, he did so.

She parted the lower half of his robe to study his legs and said, "You know, I think I could teach you to dance."

Kostas looked at her, astonished. Then he shoved some rice into his mouth with his fingers and began to chew.

"How about it?"

"I need some answers," said Kostas, his mouth full, "not distractions."

"What are your questions?"

"Who you are, for one. Where I am. How I get out of here."

"Where do you want to go?"

Kostas said nothing, not knowing.

"When you dance, questions cease."

"That's my point."

"Forget it, then." She turned and walked away without looking back.

"Wait," he called. He ran down the path and looked up, down, and to both sides, but saw no one.

That night the young woman didn't appear in his head when Kostas summoned her. He was desolate. Why had he refused her offer to teach him to dance? He had nothing else to do, possibly for the rest of his life. But it hadn't fit his scenario. He was older than she, one of New York's preeminent market analysts. She was supposed to admire him. To allow her to see him stumbling around like a newborn colt would diminish him in her eyes. It was out of the question. In any case, she was gone now. And he was glad. Why, then, did he feel so bereft? Then he became furious: He had invented her! She couldn't just decide on her own not to show up. Where the hell was she?

To his relief, she came back the next day. Settling down at his feet, she listened docilely to that day's segment of his autobiography, nodding at his triumphs, smiling at his jokes, frowning at injustices he had undergone—with only occasional yearning glances out the cave mouth. And she returned for several more weeks. Kostas concluded that she was as engrossed as he in his pilgrimage from the Slough of Queens to the Pinnacles of Great Neck. And his new happiness was rendered even more intense by the memory of his long loneliness.

One afternoon in the middle of his incantation of his college board scores, the woman stood up. "Forgive me,

Kostas, but this is too boring." She began stretching and bending in her silk shift.

Kostas watched, insulted.

She paused to look at him. "You just carry on. I'm going to limber up." So saying, she spun around his cave, swaying and writhing, leaping and crouching. The chamber filled with lilting lute music that bounced off the walls and echoed down the cavern, and her arms seemed to become feathery wings that swept and swooped as her body spun.

Kostas sat in silence munching cold rice, unable to resist occasional sideways glances at her. After a few minutes she joined the cloud of bats as they swept into the dusk, leaving Kostas in a funk, his monologue for that day interrupted, the music abruptly silenced.

The Dancer continued to visit almost daily, but now she pranced and twirled while Kostas sat in a dignified silence, recounting to himself *The Kostas Powers Story* and watching the snakes in the swamp slip slowly through the scum. He was sad: Why did she insist on fleeing the intimacy that had been giving him such pleasure? He was confused: Whenever she danced, appropriate music was piped in from nowhere. Sometimes when he glimpsed her from the corner of his eye, she appeared to be a hipless boy, a panther, a gazelle. But when he shifted his eyes for a full frontal gaze, she was merely an attractive young woman of exceptional grace. He was irritated: He never knew when she would arrive or how long she would stay, always without excuses or explanations. This was exactly why you couldn't have women on a battlefield. They were anarchists. If they didn't feel like fighting, they would refuse, regardless of what the enemy was up to. If only he possessed an appointment book and a watch, he would insist that she schedule her appearances to suit his convenience. Yet he was dazzled: How could you schedule a shooting star? Her exuberance, unsullied by any impulse toward self-defense or self-justification, was the very essence of life. And he was astonished: How could he have so little to say about someone he had created in the first place? Or had his imaginings merely drawn to him someone who approximated his blueprint, the way planting a particular flower in his Great Neck garden had always summoned the appropriate insect pest?

Realizing he was floundering in a mire of undifferentiated emotion, he decided to sort out once and for all his response to this baffling, annoying, exciting young woman. (Emotion was not Kostas's favored mode, especially several at once, and particularly if they conflicted.) With a pointed stone he wrote in the dirt all the emotions involved, and then ranked them. Since the negative ones overshadowed the positive, he decided she had to go.

The next day he yelled at her over the music as she performed a back flip that seemed to suspend her in midair, hovering like a magic hoop. "Why do you keep coming here? You're not interested in my story, and I'm not interested in your dancing."

Regaining her footing, she stood still for a moment, then said, "It's not that I'm not interested in your story, Kostas. It's just that it's the past. Whereas the present is right here before us, demanding to be lived. And I stick around because I don't enjoy *pas de une*."

"You've got lots of moves. You don't need *pas de deux*."

"Maybe not, but this job gets pretty lonely, and I could use some company out here."

"What job?"

"Dancing for people who are tone deaf."

"So switch to some other profession."

"I can't. It's what I'm good at. It's my function."

"I'm sorry, but I'm still not interested. I never was, and I never will be."

"Why don't you just try it, Kostas? Who knows, you might like it."

Kostas pondered this request, despite his disapproval of her. If only there were some way to have her buy and sell some bonds, so she would have some respect for what *he* was good at. But what the hell, why not try dancing? He had nothing to lose since he had already lost her. Furthermore, his life story had caught up to the present, making no more sense in retrospect than it had when it actually happened. Currently he was outlining in the dirt proofs for and against the existence of a God. But they appeared to cancel each other out. In any case, Kostas was a notoriously nice guy, reared to assist *pas de deux*-less maidens in distress. So he stood up and, clutching his robe, did an awkward imitation of the young woman, feeling foolish. But she proclaimed herself enchanted, and turned up the next day with a skirted tunic for him.

"But I'd look ridiculous in this," he insisted, holding it between two fingers.

"Not as ridiculous as you look with that robe flapping open."

Kostas put on the tunic in the shadows at the rear of the cave, feeling like a Roman centurion. Looking down, he discovered that it displayed his shapely legs to advantage.

The treadmill at the health club had domesticated the physical coordination Kostas had possessed on the basketball court, but under The Dancer's tutelage that innate grace began to rattle its chains. His calisthenics on the cave floor stood him in good stead as she required him to bend and stretch in ways that would have incapacitated anyone less supple. Once she was convinced his body could endure the strain, she began teaching him ballet and modern dance, the lindy and the tango, the cha cha and the samba.

One day they began trying to meld the separate tango steps into a continuous flow. After tripping, stumbling, and trampling her feet, Kostas demanded a rest. Red-faced and discouraged, he lay down. "We're not getting anywhere," he muttered.

"Where's there to get?"

He sat up and grabbed a chip of stone, with which he began to draw in the dirt. Leaning over, The Dancer discovered him diagramming their tango like a basketball play, with boxes and arrows and numbers.

She stepped back and watched him for a long time. Then she launched into a frenzied flamenco, to the clacking of phantom castanets. Moving toward him, she stamped her feet and lashed her head. As he sputtered indignantly, she trampled his drawing. Then she grabbed his hand and hauled him to his feet, placing his arms in position on her body.

Throwing aside any expectation of coherence or predictability, Kostas simply moved in unison with The Dancer, initiating movements and responding to hers as though they shared one mind. They glided back and forth across the cave, approaching and withdrawing, enticing and inciting, resisting and surrendering. The bats hanging from the ceiling swayed in their sleep, and the spider in the doorway clung to her web like a sailor to the rigging during a squall.

Afterwards, as they leaned against each other sweating and breathing heavily, The Dancer gasped, "Good job, Kostas." Her praise was never lightly offered, and Kostas felt a surge of exhilaration. He leaned over and kissed her on the mouth. His hand moved to her heaving breast, firm and round beneath the damp silk of her shift. He could taste the salt of her sweat and feel her heart pounding against his palm.

Frowning, she removed his hand.

"What's wrong?"

She stroked his hand. "Let's see, how do I explain this?" She thought for a while, then looked up at him. "To submit something that exists outside of time to the laws of time dooms it to extinction. Sometimes you have to forego something you might want in order to attain what you really need."

"Outside of time? But I thought you said you were real."

"I guess that depends on what you mean by real."

"I don't know what you're talking about," said Kostas, irritably extracting his hand. He recalled how young she was. Perhaps she was a virgin.

"I know you don't. That's why I don't know how to explain."

"You don't need to be afraid. I'd be gentle."

"I'm not afraid," she said, amused. "And what makes you believe I'd want you to be gentle?"

Kostas looked at her, shocked.

"You think this would be new for me?"

"But you exist because of me, lady. And I didn't give you a sexual past."

"I exist because of you?"

Glancing down at the scars on his arms and recalling her voice in Athens counseling him to give in, he said nothing. But damn it, he was the man. He was supposed to be doing the protecting. Yet he felt increasingly in the hands of this elusive young woman who appeared to need him not at all. So she had had other men? Maybe that was why she rarely lingered past dusk. Who were they, the slut?

"You always have to be the boss, don't you?" he muttered.

"Boss? What does that mean—boss? We don't have that word where I come from."

"Where's that?" asked Kostas, assuming correctly that he would get no answer. "Boss means the person in charge."

She looked bewildered. "But I'm in charge of me, and you're in charge of you. Why would we want to be in charge of each other? Isn't that what freedom is—recognizing and accepting and respecting each other's separateness?"

"Maybe so." Kostas was feeling less and less interested in removing this woman's silk dress. He had wanted the sensation of smooth skin against his own, not a debate on word definition. "But in real lovemaking, as two solitary selves struggle to break through the barriers, that separation can sometimes be abolished."

"Briefly."

"Yes," said Kostas, "and then you get the pleasure of doing it all over again."

"But if you achieve that union without the assistance of the flesh, then it can continue beyond the ravages of time. Call it calisthenics for the soul."

"I believe we call it death where I come from."

They sat in silence as crayfish plashed in the pool at the rear of the cave. Kostas wondered if she were waiting for him just to ignore her silly words and obscure hesitations, and take her there on the cave floor. It wasn't his style, but then neither was cave dwelling.

"If you rush love, it can turn to hate," warned The Dancer.

He looked at her. Who had said anything about the l-word? "Look, I'm sorry about my behavior just now. I'm told that lovemaking is something I'm pretty good at, and I guess I hoped if you agreed, you'd want to stick around."

"But I want to stick around in any case. Of my own free will."

"I just feel so powerless in relation to you."

She gazed into his eyes, affectionate and perplexed. "But Kostas, you can have the power. Take it. I don't want it."

He laughed. "But don't you see that since you don't care about it, you're that much more powerful?"

She frowned. "I will never understand men. Can't we be comrades? I'm no good at either ordering or obeying."

She kept coming, and they kept dancing. She maintained that Kostas was attaining an agility remarkable in a man his age. And he found himself increasingly able to dance without diagrams. Mostly he was enchanted with this new undertaking. But now and then he felt a seizure of the same panic he used to combat with Xanax. Once when he was spinning, holding her overhead with a hand in the small of her back, she seemed to slither down his arm, around his trunk, and down his leg. Then she rose up from the floor, swaying like a cobra, head darting, while the stalactites glistened and dripped.

Kostas ran to the mouth of the cave, gasping for air. But when he looked back, The Dancer was standing with her hands on her hips, astonished and concerned. He laughed weakly. "Sorry. I don't know what came over me."

Late one afternoon she arrived just as the full moon popped out of the swamp like a golden soap bubble. Although accustomed by now to her unpredictability, Kostas was annoyed because, after expecting her all day, he had finally given up and settled down to recite to the crayfish his new discourse on the non-reality of reality.

Smiling at his sulk, The Dancer said, "Come on, Kostas, you know you'd soon tire of me if I came when you called, like a pet poodle."

Kostas smiled reluctantly, and they began to dance, while silver moonbeams crept through the doorway and across the floor of packed dirt. They circled each other slowly, moving in and out, fingertips almost touching, then whisking away.

At some point Kostas realized that The Dancer's fingertips were luminescent feathers, shimmering in the moonlight. And then he saw that his own were, too. The two advanced and retreated time after time, whirling and wheeling, swooping and spinning. The candlelight cast shifting shadows on the damp stone walls, while a Pan-like piping echoed eerily.

Abruptly Kostas felt himself rise to the vaulted ceiling. Looking down, he saw himself and The Dancer, bathed in white light, wing tips dipping.

And then he was outside the cave, drifting upward, spiraling as though performing a basketball layup in slow motion. He felt a flicker of fear. But within his head he heard The Dancer saying, "Let go, Kostas. Give up. Give in." And he realized that she was with him. Not beside him, but inside him, and he inside her. Or neither inside either, since there was no longer a him or a her. Instead, they formed a single awareness, each discrete yet not separate, like the lobes of a leaf. They hung suspended in space, looking down at the mountain of stone with its honeycombed caves, at the black lagoon with its snoozing snakes.

Soon the lagoon was just a tiny ink blot on a viridian island that was floating on a milky turquoise sea. This sea encircled a sphere that gradually shrank to the size of a cat-eye marble, with shiny silver caps of ice at each pole. And all around Kostas, like motes in a sunbeam, drifted thousands of sparkling pinpoints of light, suns to millions of such bright shining marbles. He heard a pulsing hum that seemed to swell until it filled this firmament....

Kostas felt the moment fading. He felt it fade and he let it go. He was just a wick, he realized, not the flame. But he now understood that a flame needs a wick just as much as a wick needs the flame. His eyes swam as though he had been staring directly into the flame. And he shuddered slowly, with fear and with amazement, to realize that he himself had hosted the flame. He had been warmed and scorched and burned by the flame. For a brief moment he had *been* the flame.

Kostas found himself crumpled on the cave floor in his sweaty tunic, The Dancer beside him in her soiled silk. She opened her eyes and looked at him.

"Gosh," he said.

She smiled faintly.

They stood up and straightened out their clothing, while silver fingers of moonlight softly probed the recesses of the cave and stroked the albino crayfish as they slept.

"Do you notice anything different about me?" Kostas finally asked.

"What, your wings?"

"Yes, my wings!" He laughed. "You sound so unimpressed."

"They've always been there. I wondered when you'd notice." She walked toward the doorway.

"But you can't go now!"

"Especially now. Presence and absence—it's a necessary oscillation. Don't worry. I'll be back."

"But when?" He stared at her, horrified.

"When it's time."

"When will that be?"

"I don't know."

"But after all that, I thought you'd finally stay for good."

"What, and stand in the doorway to greet you home from hunting in the swamp?"

"I had hoped you might. Please don't go. I need you."

"But Kostas, I'm always with you."

"I mean really here."

She sighed. "You seem to want to possess what can only be freely given."

"But I love you," he was alarmed to hear himself confess.

"I love you too. But if it's not a continually renewed choice, it's not a bond, it's bondage." She turned to go.

In desperation he grabbed her wing. "Dancer, I'm sick of your word games." He pulled her to him and felt her body yield. Her mouth opened to his.

But just as abruptly she turned her head aside and pushed him away. "That's not what this is all about, Kostas."

"Damn it, you've teased me enough." He put his hands on her hips and forced her against himself. He had never in his life had to ask for sex, much less beg for it. He wondered what to do next.

The Dancer solved his problem by vanishing, leaving behind only a couple of feathers, which floated to the dirt floor.

Kostas plopped down, breathing heavily, while the moon disappeared behind the mountain wall, plunging the swamp into blackness. The flickering candle flame threw umbral images across the slick cave walls.

It was one thing to dwell in the dark when you had never known light, he realized. The crayfish had hatched albino. But to have drifted in the moonlight in The Dancer's embrace rendered this cave a dungeon. The hooded hangman had slipped up on him unawares, disguised as a young woman in a silk shift, so at ease on her feet that fluff from a milkweed pod on an autumn gust would have seemed ponderous. Kostas had learned to dance to please her. But she had gone away, leaving him behind to grovel in the dust, not part of her world but estranged now from his own. He began to cry, great rasping sobs of grief and frustration, like a child whose balloon has been swept away on a gust of wind.

Leaning over, he wiped his tears on his skirt. Then he struggled to his feet. He would prove to them both that he didn't need her. Shakily he attempted the moves he had performed with such virtuosity earlier in the evening—and found he could do them without her. And his arms were still covered with feathers that scintillated in the starlight.

For what seemed like hours he whirled and wheeled. Yet each time he sensed that he was about to rise to the ceiling, he congratulated himself so heartily on his self-sufficiency that the possibility passed.

Eventually he concluded that he didn't want to be drifting around the stratosphere anyway, especially since it involved surrendering everything that made him Kostas—his independence, his shrewd intelligence, even his physical form as he had always known it. Like Calypso, The Dancer was trying to trap him here in this cave for her own gratification, heedless of what his own destiny might involve.

As the evening progressed, the nature of his dancing shifted, and the music with it—from mellow haunting woodwinds to throbbing drums and stabbing brass. Sweat trickled down his chest and dripped from his beard. His basketball knee ached as his feet stamped and pawed, as his torso twisted and writhed in a savage salute to rage and despair.

For a moment the candlelight playing on the moist stones resembled a swaying serpent. In a frenzy of anguish, Kostas broke a stalactite from the ceiling and hurled it like a spear at the vaporous viper.

As an angry red dawn stained his newfound wings with blood, Kostas knew it was time to leave this mountainside above the swamp. When The Dancer deigned to reappear, she would find only a vacant cave piled high with bat dung. He couldn't wait to get back to Penny, a real woman, one eager to bake casseroles to celebrate his return, one happy to take him into her arms and gaze into his eyes, one eager to mold her body to his and stroke his rejected flesh. As he exited, Kostas ripped the shimmering web from the doorway with a single sweep of one wing, hurling the spider into the stream at the rear of the cave, where the crayfish were unable to save her from a whirlpool that sucked her into the hollow center of the massive mountain.

Kostas found Penny, dressed in black Spandex bicycle shorts and a powder blue Jog Bra, necking in the kitchen of the Great Neck house with a young thug sporting a foot-high flattop, and a Confederate flag tattoo on his forearm. He felt a flash of rage: his wife in his kitchen! His fists clenched. Looking at them, Kostas recalled hurling the stalactite at the shadow in the cave. What was this? He had never been a fighter. He had always believed in reason. Besides, he had been without possessions for so long now that it seemed a trifle histrionic to regard Penny and this kitchen as "his." And he had scarcely been Spouse of the Year himself. No doubt she would boot her young stud out now that her husband was home.

Penny paused to look at Kostas in his tattered tunic. She didn't recognize him.

"Uh, could you give me something to eat?"

"Help yourself at the buffet table," she said doubtfully. "We're having a clam bake."

Dodging a golden retriever that was leaping up to catch a flying Frisbee, Kostas reached the picnic table and piled a plate high with barbecued ribs, coleslaw, and baked beans. Evidently Penny's ethnic fascination had shifted from Kostas's Greek heritage to that of her new paramour. Sitting in the sand eating his first non-rice meal in years, Kostas spotted Mike among the volleyballers, slamming the ball over the net. Mike also spotted him and yelled, "Well, look who's back!" He jogged over.

"Thank God you're home, " said Mike as they embraced. "Mom's flipped out. She's opened a weaving studio and has started an affair with some dude from a singles bar."

"I saw him. Nice hairdo."

"I'd watch out for him, Dad. He's bound to have some Oedipal issues with you."

"You finished your psychology program?" guessed Kostas.

"Yes, and I have my own therapy practice now. Hey, Mom! Guess who's here!"

STORMY WEATHER AND OTHER STORIES

Penny was strolling from the house with a platter of sliced watermelon. She studied Kostas again and finally said, "Well, my lord, Kostas. I'd given up on you."

"So I see." He nodded at the smiling young hoodlum by her side.

She shrugged sheepishly.

Kostas sat before the driftwood fire with Penny and Luther, who drove a refrigerated truck for Stouffer's. It looked serious: Luther was wearing a tee shirt on which Penny had silk-screened a Harley emblem, and they were taking Dirty Dancing lessons together at the Great Neck Y. They stood up and joined the young people writhing in the sand to the Eurhythmics. Penny slid up and down Luther's black leather thigh in her Spandex bicycle shorts like a merry-go-round horse on its pole.

Kostas felt a stab of misery as he spat watermelon seeds into the flames. He had apparently lost Penny. But maybe it wasn't too late? Struggling to his feet, he spread his wings and began to strut. It was one of his finer performances, and the entire clambake froze in place to watch. The retriever barked furiously, as though at a seagull. The neighbor's young daughter tugged at her mother's sleeve, pointing at his wings. She even tried to imitate Kostas, swaying and swirling her skinny arms. But no one else seemed to notice his transformation.

Penny picked her way through the flying sand to his side. With a concerned gaze she took his arm and led him toward the house, calling to the crowd with strained gaiety, "You know Kostas. He never does anything halfway. He has a midlife crisis, so he hits the road for three years. He goes to Greece and comes home as Zorba! Come along, honey. You need some rest. Also a bath!" Everyone laughed good-humoredly and resumed the lambada around the bonfire.

Luther said to Kostas, "Man, you know, there's a twelve-step program for whatever ails you right here in Great Neck."

Penny slipped her arm around Kostas's waist and said, "Don't worry, dear. Everything's going to be all right. Tomorrow we'll renew your Xanax prescription."

Kostas lay in Mike's old bedroom listening to gasps and groans of sexual fulfillment from the master bedroom. Apparently you couldn't go home again because what you had left behind was no longer yours. But he didn't even want Penny anymore, he realized. The only woman he wanted was The Dancer, and that was finished. She had unmanned him, as Delilah had Samson, flirting shamelessly in her clinging silk shift, until he agreed to prance around a cave in a miniskirt. He had passed his days waiting for her in his tunic like a housewife in her apron. He had traded in muscled arms for feathered wings. He had lain weeping in the dirt like a heartbroken girl. And he hadn't even gotten properly laid for his efforts. If the universe was really one continuum, how could The Dancer amputate their bodies from the neck down? Clearly she was on some weird ascetic trip, and he was lucky to have escaped with only a broken heart.

But he had truly loved her, he insisted to his pillow, more than she had him, despite her stance of expertise on the subject. Hadn't he sacrificed his career, his wife, his house, his belongings, his nation to remain there in the cave with her? Yes, and he had opened himself up to her as she had not to him, taking on her passion for dance as his own. He recalled that he still had his wings, and all the moves The Dancer had taught him. Maybe he could take them on the road and earn enough change to feed himself while he figured out what to do next. Then, at least this blighted love of theirs wouldn't have been a complete waste of time.

"Not yet, Kostas," said a voice in his head. "It's too soon."

Stunned to hear her for the first time since she vanished from the cave, he said nothing. Hope flickered in his heart. Maybe he hadn't alienated her forever? But she resumed her silence. And then Kostas remembered all her other silences and absences.

"Go away, Dancer. You've hurt me enough." He turned toward the wall, wrapped his head in the pillow, and tried to sleep.

Kostas began to dance in the shadow of his semi-circular glass office building, dodging broken bottles and cast-off hotdogs, with ferries to Staten Island and memorials to immigrant forebears as a backdrop. Eventually a few passersby paused to watch. Kostas recognized some young people from his office, though they appeared not to know him in his tunic. People brought their friends and the crowd grew. A street musician offered to provide saxophone accompaniment. Performances started to elicit applause. Enthusiastic supporters collected donations on his behalf.

Before long Battery Park was jammed at lunch hour with bankers, brokers, secretaries, and temps, all eager to see Kostas. And soon the windows of the buildings around the park and the balconies at the ferry pier teemed with spectators. Private yachts moored offshore, and the Circle Line added to their itinerary a stop for Kostas's performance. Women marveled over his legs and enrolled protesting husbands in dance classes. The *New York Magazine* dance critic wrote, "Not since Nureyev have we seen such virility yoked to such grace. Kostas Powers is the greatest American dancer since Fred Astaire."

All the perquisites of instant fame were his: Groupies invited him to Roseland. A producer asked to option his film rights. Con men tried to sell him offshore oil rigs. A psychopath shot a hole through one of his wings.

Almost overnight Kostas had made it in the Big Apple, that cold cruel city that swallows people's dreams as Noah's whale did sailors. And Kostas ate it for breakfast, recalling his days as a basketball star. Occasionally a small voice in his head attempted to be heard over the roar of the crowd: "Watch out, Kostas. You are but a man." Yet Kostas did his best not to hear, believing The Dancer to be simply envious of his success.

None of the critics mentioned his wings, but babies in strollers giggled, pointed, and burbled baby talk for "bird" at puzzled parents. Dog walkers learned to avoid the park altogether after a pack of bird dogs broke free and attempted to chase down Kostas in mid-strut. Alley cats paused with fish market offal to hiss at Kostas with flashing yellow eyes and flexing claws. Seagulls stopped fighting over pretzels on the promenade to line the bench backs and watch their brother bird in concert. Black falcons swooped down from their aeries atop luxury high-rises to observe silently from the immigrant monuments.

Meanwhile, Kostas's human audiences tapped their toes and swayed their torsos, bobbed their heads to the beat and shouted encouragement like the saved at revivals. They believed they were being entertained. But like yeast in dough, the dance began to have an unforeseen effect. One by one people became aware of his wings, and so powerful was this illusion of a creature half-animal and half-angel that they had to question the dependability of their senses. Those who had been hippies in the sixties were enchanted, and got out their old love beads and pot pipes. Others ceased to attend, complaining that they had seen it all before. Some who stuck it out fell silent and troubled, sensing that reality might not be as reliable as it had once seemed. They knew from *People Magazine* that Kostas had been a simple bond trader from Great Neck. He had had arms for grasping and hitting, not wings for soaring. A few wondered if they too might learn to dance, but most had no wish for wings in place of arms, for how would they take out the garbage or punch a time clock or drive in rush-hour traffic?

One afternoon Kostas was whirling in and out among the huge concrete tablets that listed sailors lost at sea during World War II. The Statue of Liberty loomed before him, and the World Trade Center at his back. He was catching glimpses of his swirling feathers in the glass wall of his former office building. Pacing himself to the remembered rhythms of that night when he and The Dancer had achieved union with the universe, he was allowing the tension to mount by degrees, containing it, reeling it out like a hooked marlin, then reining it in. He and the assembled crowd would experience as one that breakthrough into another dimension, and life on earth would be forever altered. Kostas would join Tolstoy and Ghandi, Darwin and Freud and Einstein, Martin Luther King and John Kennedy in the ranks of advance scouts along the trail toward a new world order. History classes would resound with his name and that day's date.

"Forget it, Kostas. Quit now while you're ahead," cautioned a voice in his head, which he ignored.

So busy was Kostas watching his graceful reflection in the glass office building, and picturing this same image, larger than life, looming over Times Square on a neon billboard, that he missed a beat. He stumbled. He fell. And the universe appeared to falter like a bicycle pedal slipping a cog. The ground trembled, shattering the wall of glass. Slivers showered down and impaled pedestrians below. The sky darkened to the hue of a clotted wound. Stabs of lightning ignited oil tanks across the water in Bayonne. Falcons swooped down to carry off shrieking pigeons. Fighter planes screamed overhead, and enemy submarines torpedoed tour boats by the pier. Kostas watched helplessly, unable to return to the bottle the genie he had unwittingly unleashed, while the building of crazed glass reflected the contused sky.

In the stunned silence that followed, the members of the terrified audience clutched one another's hands and gazed toward the blood-red bay. A gondola poled by a poker-faced Charon floated past Kostas up the Hudson, leaving no wake. And all the people in the park understood as one that sooner or later each would suffer horribly and die alone, even though all had secretly expected exemption. One day the Twin Towers of the World Trade Center would topple like a toddler's Legos, and bloated corpses would clog the harbors. The deserted halls of Lincoln Center would swarm with roaches and colonies of ravenous rats. Tattered dollar bills would swirl down Fifth Avenue and pile up in soggy heaps by the storm drains. Lap dogs gone wild would howl as the tip of the Chrysler Building impaled a bruised and swollen moon. And all the VCRs and microwave ovens, the synthetic furs and luxury sedans would be carried out to sea on a riptide of blood.

As this vision faded, everyone remained silent. Eventually people wandered off alone or in couples, wondering what was the point in doing this rather than that. What was the point in doing anything at all? And finally all hell broke loose, with fickle fans hurling roasted chestnuts at Kostas. The saxophone player walked over to say, "Burn out time, man. Better give it all a rest."

Kostas sat on a slotted bench in the park reading in the *Times* that he danced "with all the grace and energy of a fatigued Quasimodo." Squirrels in the maples were showering him with peanut shells, and a play group was pelting him with gravel. In the space of a few weeks' time a star had been born and extinguished, a time-lapse supernova. One misstep and his career lay in ruins. He would never dance again. Yet after all he had experienced in the cave and since, he knew he could never return to the tedium of that shattered glass building in the shadow of which he was now sitting. What was left for him, apart from a stolen embrace with the third rail?

"Lighten up, Kostas," suggested The Dancer as she shooed away the scornful squirrels and sat down beside him in her silk shift.

"Get outa my face." He refused to look at her, afraid of ripping the fragile scabs off his wounded heart.

"Don't take it so hard. You're in good company: Isaiah and Jeremiah. Cotton Mather. Oral Roberts. What could be bad?" As she patted his shoulder, he twitched it irritably to one side.

"Why didn't you warn me?"

"You know perfectly well that I warned you until I was blue in the face."

"Why didn't you stop me?"

"Haven't you ever heard of free will? People do what they do, and then mop up afterwards."

"If you hadn't left me alone in that cave, none of this would have happened." He wadded up the dance page of the *Times* and lofted it into the trash basket.

"Right. So it's all my fault."

"I never wanted to dance in the first place. I'm sorry I ever met you." He lifted his head and allowed himself a glance at her. She was just a skinny kid with a cowlick and a pointed nose. How could he have ever sobbed in the dirt over such a dog?

"It's not my blue-ribbon moment either. But no doubt we deserve each other. There are many apparent injustices in this universe, but no accidents."

"What do you call what just happened?"

"I call it hubris. Every coin has a flip side. Eros and Thanatos. You should have waited until your lantern was burning brightly enough for a descent into the pit. And you should never have taken along day trippers."

"Dancer, is there anything you don't know?"

"I don't know." She giggled.

"Ha, ha. Very funny." He scowled, to illustrate that her charm would no longer work on him.

"Never mind. Let's get busy. We'll pick up where we left off." She jumped up.

Kostas was swept with relief. She still wanted him? Then he recalled how she wanted him—as her sycophant, her lackey. He hadn't escaped the dominion of his mother and Penny simply to submit to another bossy woman.

"Come on." She grabbed his wing tip.

He swept his wing away. "I'm not dancing anymore."

"Nonsense." She dragged him to his feet.

"You're too skinny." He inspected her. "You look like a boy."

"So what? What does that have to do with dancing?"

"I've told you: I'm finished with dancing. So go away." He shoved her so hard that she fell to the sidewalk, where she sat looking up at him disbelievingly. He delivered a karate kick to her jaw that laid her out flat. Then he stomped her until she was bruised and bleeding, while several old men on nearby benches, chins resting on fists, watched without comment. She put up no resistance. Kostas felt his wings dissolving.

After a moment of distress he knelt down and wrapped his reconstituted hands around her throat, watching her startled face take on hues of blue and purple, like a dying fish. He had thought she was an angel of light, but it was now clear that she was a demon of the dark who had to be destroyed. He wrenched the grate off a subway vent and dumped The Dancer's broken body into it. Defeathered arms limp by his sides, Kostas strode from the park, reassured to know that that creature from hell now lay in a clammy tunnel, about to be sliced to bits by sharp tires, pissed on by bums, and devoured by rats.

Behind him he heard a husky voice: "Not so fast, jerk off."

Turning, he saw The Dancer, attired in a breastplate and helmet, sword in one hand. "I thought I killed you," he gasped.

She laughed. "Dream on, big man. Play fair this time."

She threw Kostas some armor. They went at it for hours, slashing and lunging, slicing and stabbing, as though again dancing the tango. The Dancer seemed to assume different shapes as they struggled, with writhing snakes for hair and hollow eyes weeping blood. To Kostas it was Armageddon, a fight for his very life against the massed forces of evil. The clashing of their swords drew a crowd of office workers munching deli sandwiches. Sometimes Kostas would kneel on her chest, sword at her throat, only to be hurled off. And vice versa. They yelled, grunted, and screamed.

Finally The Dancer faltered, looking into Kostas's fierce blue eyes through his helmet visor with amused affection. Kostas took advantage of this moment of tenderness to plunge his sword through a gap in her breastplate, up to its hilt.

As she lay there dying, The Dancer gasped, "Kostas, I should warn you that it's not this easy to get rid of me."

"Once I'm finished, you'll never dance again," he hissed, withdrawing his sword to flood the pavement with her blood.

"Despite everything, I am fond of you," she whispered as her eyes clouded over like those of the dying gull at Kostas's office window when his endless nightmare had first begun.

With one stroke of his sword, Kostas sliced her body in half. In a benumbed trance he ripped out her heart and hurled it to a nearby schnauzer. Methodically he chopped each half into chunks, which he dumped into a trashcan reading "Let's Clean Up New York." Throwing off his armor and helmet, he vaulted the iron fence into the Hudson and swam out to meet an ocean-going cargo ship, as police sirens whooped through the narrow streets.

Kostas sat in his cabin while the boat surged and swayed, drinking Madeira and recalling the graceful young woman in her clinging silk gown who had entered his cave one day with the promise of infinite accord. They had experienced together the harmony of the spheres. What had gone wrong? It was like the collapse of a soufflé. All you could do was throw it out. But why did he have to kill someone whom he had loved more than anyone else in his entire life? He, who had been a manager, negotiator, father, husband, protector, provider, was also a murderer. The full horror of what he had done dawned on him gradually, and he began to drink steadily. If only she were still alive, he would dance with her until his legs fell off.

His chin sank to his chest, and he rolled from his chair onto the floor, where he descended into a wine-soaked stupor.

When he awoke in the morning to the sound of swells soughing against the side of the ship, he considered joining the French Foreign Legion once they docked at Tangiers. He could burn down villages and live in a tent with other warriors, in order to erase the memory of that Valkyrie who had tricked him into performing ballet in a tunic. He had lost himself by dancing in a moonlit grotto. Perhaps he could retrieve himself by fighting under a scorching desert sun? Some deeds of heroism might annul the sensations of longing, helplessness, irrelevance, and humiliation to which she had reduced him.

That night he dreamed he was back in the cave with The Dancer. She was healthy and whole, as insufferable as ever. They were waltzing in evening clothes to soaring, swirling strings, and sipping champagne from sloshing glasses, characters in a thirties film.

"Well, Kostas," she said amiably, "since you can't run the show in here, no doubt you'll need to run it everywhere else."

"You may know how to dance, but I know how to destroy the dancer. So who's actually running the show?"

They both laughed merrily and sipped their bubbly champagne.

"You can kill the dancer, " said she, "but never the dance."

"Watch me." He swept her out the cave mouth and pushed her off the cliff into the swamp.

But before she reached the water, she turned into a white heron and swooped away over the tangled treetops into the fiery dawn.

As the Canary Islands appeared on the horizon, Kostas was sitting in a deck chair guzzling from a jug of Madeira and reading *The Story of O*. If only he had thought to chain The Dancer to the cave wall by a ring through her labia, he reflected as he gazed across the rolling blue ocean. He should have taken charge, shown her who was boss. All women craved a boot on their chests.

He spotted a V-shaped wake cutting across the sea, moving rapidly toward the ship. As it drew alongside, he discovered that it was produced by a huge finned serpent perhaps forty feet long. Its black scales glistened purple, green, and gold in the sun as several slithering humps broke the surface of the ultramarine sea. In astonishment he watched the body slide beneath the keel. Then a head shaped like a Brazil nut appeared above the gunwale on a long arched neck that swayed with the swells. Kostas stared speechlessly into the lidless yellow eyes.

"Can we talk?" it asked.

"Christ, it's you!" He felt horror and relief, rage and remorse, all at once. Was this another dream? Hallucinations from all the alcohol? Grabbing the jug, he swallowed half a liter of wine in several gulps.

The monster's lipless mouth appeared to smile, and the reptilian nostrils flared.

"Can't you just leave me alone?" he groaned, shoving the cork back into the bottle.

"I could, but then where would you be? You're deteriorating at an incredible clip without me around to keep you human."

Kostas laughed so hard that *The Story of O* fell off his lap onto the deck. "Have you looked in a mirror lately, Dancer?"

"I am as you conceive me to be."

"Good. I conceive you to be history. So get lost."

Nodding at his reading matter, she said, "I'd call you a beast if it weren't an insult to the animal kingdom."

Kostas felt sheepish, remembering his mother finding *Penthouse* beneath his mattress when he was a boy. Then he noticed that while they had been talking, she had been coiling her shiny black body around the bow as though preparing to drag the ship to the bottom of the sea. Leaping up, he seized a harpoon from the cabin wall and thrust it through one coil, pinning her to the forecastle.

"That just proves my point," gasped The Dancer as fluid gushed from her wound.

"Beat it, lady." Kostas repeated the harpoon procedure at several more sites, like a banderillero run amuck.

The Dancer raised her head weakly to flare a milk-white hood and display several pointed fangs dripping venom. "I didn't intend to hurt you, Kostas. I guess you weren't ready. I'm sorry. I thought you understood what was going on."

"I understood it my way. And you'd never explain yours." Kostas was on the verge of tears, so he grabbed a fire axe and planted it in the monster's writhing body. How could an appealing young woman have been transformed into this repulsive sea slug? He had to get rid of this protean creature once and for all, and get back to a land where men were men, women were women, birds were birds, monsters were monsters....

The caravan of soldiers, cartridge belts crossed atop their khaki uniforms, pistols on their hips, halted in a grove of date palms at the foot of a rocky pass between two peaks. Basketball knee aching from his days in the saddle, Kostas limped over to the well in his high black boots. Beside it stood a young woman, robed and veiled, with an orange clay pitcher on her head. Silently she offered it to him. Taking it, he emptied it down his parched throat. As he was wiping his mouth on his sleeve, his eyes met hers. She lifted her filmy veil, but not before Kostas had scrutinized her clear, candid expression.

"Dancer?" he whispered, feeling a surge of joy.

She nodded, the pitcher trembling in her hands.

His arms rose of their own accord to embrace her. In confusion he lowered them to his sides, but he greedily drank in her steady, loving gaze while the sun burned down and the stallions stamped and snorted and a cricket chirped from the cool well wall.

"It's not my nature to offer explanations," said the monster, pinned to the ship's deck like a chloroformed insect by the harpoons. Its nostrils were spewing gore.

"And it's not my nature to dance ballet in a tunic. I submitted to you because I loved you. But I can assure you this will never happen again." Kostas was waving his arms frantically to summon the deck hands.

"There's a difference between surrender and submission."

"That's one thing I always hated most about you, Dancer—your preoccupation with semantics."

Sorrowfully she shook her saurian head. "This is a real mess. But we can sort it out."

"I just want to be left alone," he muttered, lashing her fins to a mast with a rope.

He paused to watch with dismay as the wounds he had dealt her bathed the decks with blood. He had been praying in his cabin for another chance, yet here he went again. He just couldn't seem to stop killing her.

"I can't keep this up much longer, Kostas," said the young woman by the well, lowering her veil to reveal a quavering smile, at once brave yet tentative.

"Don't," he said earnestly. "Please just go home, Dancer, wherever that may be. Forget about me. It's finished. I'm no good for you."

"How could I ever forget you, Kostas?"

Kostas could feel his heart straining to burst out of his chest and join hers in that enchanted land they had begun to chart together. But he had heeded this heart once, and it had yielded helplessness and humiliation.

"Allow me to make this easier for you, Dancer." His blue eyes turned dull and listless, and his cracked lips set themselves in a thin, tight line. He flipped the metal lid off the well and swept her up in his muscled arms.

"Kostas, please don't do this." The pitcher fell from her hands and shattered on the ground.

Kostas hesitated, looking down at the lovely young woman in his arms. Why not accept her, live with her, learn from her, love her? Then he recalled that she could never really be his. She was merely an enticing illusion, one who would always come and go as she pleased, leaving him behind with a handful of feathers and a heart full of hurt. Kostas dropped The Dancer down the dark hole, replaced the lid, and ran to his pawing stallion, cartridge belts clanking.

"What are you so afraid of, Kostas?" asked the monster, thrashing weakly against the harpoons as Kostas skidded across the deck in a puddle of blood.

"I am afraid of nothing," he assured her, wresting free a lifeboat and lowering it to the water.

"You'll never escape me," called the monster in a faint voice. "Like a beach ball I'll keep popping up, higher and higher the deeper you push me under."

Kostas jumped into the boat and rowed away like an Olympian sculler, while the monster struggled with the panicked sailors, who were now blasting her serpentine body with AK-47s. From a distance, Kostas paused to watch her flayed carcass sink beneath the waves. As an armada of sharks in a feeding frenzy turned the sea into a cauldron of gore, Kostas buried his face in his hands and wept.

The Dancer wiped algae from her eyes and touched the moist stone wall of the well with her fingertips. As she treaded water, she began to cry, tears dripping off her chin. Let him go, she whispered in the blackness. Give up. Give in. It was no use. He was gone. She was alone. Both were lost. The dancing was done. Kostas had won.

The churning of her legs began to slow, and the water rose—to her shoulders, to her throat, to her lips. The alarmed cricket chirruped from its hideout among the mossy stones.

Light was pouring down from above. Looking up, she saw golden sun and blue sky where the heavy metal lid had been. And a dangling rope held by two strong fists. And a luminous face with an aureole of curly hair. Impossible to tell if it were a man or a woman, but the friendly eyes conveyed competence and compassion.

"I'll get you out, Dancer. Grab hold," said the young person, the sonorous voice echoing off the damp stones.

The Dancer hesitated, contemplating all the bad decisions of her recent past. But finally she shrugged off the sodden robe that was dragging her under. Reaching up, she seized the rope, and felt the slack disappear.

ACKNOWLEDGMENTS

Special thanks to the following people: George Brosi of *Appalachian Heritage* and John Lang of the *Iron Mountain Review* for featuring "The Fox Hunt" and "The Eye of the Lord" in special editions of their journals, and for their many years of support for Appalachian writing and writers; Douglas Paschall, Alice Swanson, the late Elaine Koster, Joseph Pittman, and William Shore for selecting stories of mine for their anthologies; Francoise Gilot for creating and sharing with me her haunting monotype series that inspired my novella, *Birdman and the Dancer*; Georg Heepe at Rowohlt Publishers in Hamburg, Harko Keijzer at Contact Publishers in Amsterdam, and Johannes Riis at Gyldendal Publishers in Copenhagen, for first publishing *Birdman and the Dancer* with some of the Gilot monotypes; Marc Jolley, Marsha Luttrell, and all the wonderful folks at Mercer University Press for designing, producing, and publishing this collection; David Carriere, Barbara Keene, and Mary Beth Kosowski for their help in introducing it to interested readers; and Ina Danko for her unstinting support of me and my work.